THE VISCOUNT'S CHRISTMAS QUEEN: A REGENCY ROMANCE

CHRISTMAS KISSES (BOOK 2)

ROSE PEARSON

THE VISCOUNT'S CHRISTMAS QUEEN

That was a very severe mishap. One that I cannot allow myself to ever make again.

Lucius, the Earl of Northwick, winced as he shook his head to himself, running one hand over his eyes before setting his elbow down on the arm of the chair and dropping his head into it. He was idle. In fact, he had been idle for some time, to the point that his mind was currently thinking about all that had taken place during the summer Season, rather than considering what he might do at the present to entertain himself.

Another heavy sigh emitted from his lips as he dropped his head back, looking up at the ceiling. Nothing seemed to give him any joy, save for thinking on how excellent the summer had been. Rising from his chair, he made his way across the drawing room, put both hands on the windowsill, rounded his shoulders, and dropped his head as a long breath escaped from him.

Outside, it was cold and grey, with sleet and snow beginning to pelt the frozen ground. There was no color anywhere, it seemed, nothing that would lift his spirits. The cold air reached out from behind the glass toward him, its icy chill wrapping around his shoulders and making him shudder.

The summer Season was nothing but a distant memory now, and as Lucius considered that, yet another sigh broke from him. How long would it be until he could go to London again? The summer months always seemed to pass far too quickly, and the winter months dragged out far too long. He could already feel the weight of the grey dark days tying themselves around his neck, weighing him down and tugging his spirits low.

"And I do not even have my own mother for company."

Muttering to himself, Lucius drew in a long breath. His mother had already written to him, stating she would be spending the winter months – including her Christmas – with some dear friends. Lucius was not invited to join them, and while he was glad his mother had some close friendships, he did feel her absence all the same. There came a loneliness with spending his time alone in the manor house with only the servants for company. He could not even go riding when the weather was so disastrous.

Closing his eyes, Lucius scowled to himself. This was the time of year when everything seemed to move a good deal more slowly. There were very few invitations, hardly any gatherings, and with the weather as poor as it was at present, Lucius was trapped within his own four walls. Yes, there was always some business to attend to and he could certainly look at his plans for his crops for the spring and the summertime... but none of it was as good as enjoying some pleasant company.

Shoving both hands through his fair hair, Lucius made his way back to his chair and slumped back down within it. Surely there was something he could do to remove this dreariness from his soul? But what was there to do when one was in the midst of the cold, dark winter?

Nothing. Absolutely nothing.

The summer Season had been an excellent one, albeit with the odd difficulty here and there. He had been able to push that aside easily enough and now his thoughts lingered on the joys and the laughter, the music, and the conversation – only for his gaze to look out at the view before him, reminding him of the bleak winter he was now left with. He had considered going to London for the winter Season but had decided against it. Winter in London was a very different affair from the summertime in London. It held some enjoyment, certainly, but it could not be compared to the summer Season. There would be fewer of his acquaintances, fewer of his close friends present, and everything would be very cold, grey, and damp. Such things would not lift his spirits, although, now that he let out yet another broken sigh, Lucius wondered silently if he had made the wrong decision.

A scratch at the door alerted him to the presence of one of his staff. Turning, he called for them to enter and the butler stepped inside, inclining his head as he did so. A silver tray was in his hand as he stopped just inside the room.

"My lord, you have a letter."

Lucius pushed himself up in his chair, and allowed the faint surprise in his chest to spread across his features. "A letter?"

"Yes, my lord."

He blinked in surprise. It was not the time of year to receive letters, for the winter was very cold and there had recently been a great deal of snow on the ground. It was even snowing at this present moment, was it not? Correspondence had become infrequent for, in these last few weeks, Lucius had only received one letter from his solicitors, another from his mother, and one final one from his man of business, who was presently inspecting the Dower house.

"Who is it from?"

The butler said nothing, and Lucius rolled his eyes to himself, irritated at his own foolishness. Of course the butler would not know – or if he did, he certainly would not admit it!

"I shall take it at once." Getting to his feet, he crossed the room as the butler came toward him also so that they met in the middle of the room. Lucius caught the slight flash in the butler's eyes, and his irritation at his own behavior grew all the more. His staff did not need to know that he had become a little melancholy of late.

With a wave of his hand to dismiss the butler, Lucius turned the letter over quickly. Studying the seal for a few moments, his breath hitched at the slight lift of anticipation that filled his chest. The letter was from someone of great importance, for he was quite certain that the seal was that of the Duke of Meyrick. Carefully, he unfolded the letter, letting his gaze run down over the page.

"Yes, I am correct!" Excitement flooded him as his gaze drifted over the swirling letters from the Duke of Merrick. Yes, the gentleman had written to him, which meant this must be an invitation of some kind.

Murmuring the words aloud, Lucius read over the letter once, twice, and then a third time as a broad smile broke across his features, his heart tugging free of the melancholy that had held it for so long. It seemed as though he was not to spend the winter on his own without anyone for company! The Duke of Meyrick was to have a house party

– a prolonged one, it seemed – and Lucius was invited to join the house party whenever he wished, if he was eager to attend.

"Of course I am eager," he murmured, closing his eyes for a moment. "This is the most excellent news."

Opening his eyes, Lucius crossed the room, filled a glass with a good measure of brandy, and took a long sip. Warmth flooded him, seeming to send life into his limbs and yet further joy into his heart as he once more read the letter from the Duke. His anticipation began to grow as he strode across the room to the door, flinging it open wide so that he might hurry along the hallway, making his way directly to the study.

"I am not to be disturbed." Flinging his determined words to the startled footman who stood guard by his study door, Lucius shut it tightly and locked it for good measure. He did not want to be interrupted while he wrote his letter of acceptance to the Duke.

It must be worded properly.

Setting the invitation down on his desk and placing the glass of brandy alongside it, Lucius took a moment to sit down at the table and consider what he might say. Pulling out a fresh sheet of paper, he found his ink bottle and his quill and began to write.

It took him three attempts before he was happy with how he had expressed himself. Reading it one final time, he sanded the letter and then immediately folded it up. It took a few moments for his wax and seal to be ready, but once they were completed, Lucius' task was finished. Getting out of his chair, he strode across the room and, after unlocking it, yanked open the door.

"That must be sent at once. Without delay. At this very moment. Do you understand?"

The footman started in surprise but took the letter from Lucius with a murmur of understanding. He turned sharply and walked hurriedly along the hallway as Lucius looked after him, his arms folded across his chest and a broad grin now settling in his expression – a smile he did not think would leave him for some time yet.

"I am to go to the Duke of Meyrick's house party."

Even saying such a thing brought such a great joy to Lucius' heart that he wanted to jump in the air and exclaim aloud. In an instant, his winter had been turned from shadow to bright light. No doubt there would be many of his acquaintances there, games, dinners, and even dancing. Everything he had been missing was now being presented to him – and he only had a week or so to wait.

All the more delighted, he turned back toward his study, pushing the door closed behind him as he went in search of his brandy. Taking another sip, he raised it in a toast as though the Duke of Meyrick were there with him, able to see and appreciate the toast that Lucius was offering him.

"May this be an excellent Christmas." Lucius grinned to the empty room, suddenly having a great appreciation for the crackling fire in the grate and for the lightly falling snow outside. It did not matter to him whether or not the snow was heavy or even if the roads were considered dangerous. When the time came, he would make his way to the Duke of Meyrick's house one way or the other. Nothing would prevent him, nothing would keep him back from attending the Duke of Meyrick's Christmas house party.

*L*ucius took a long draught of his brandy and let out a lengthy, contented sigh. "This is just what I need. I cannot tell you how much I appreciate being here."

His friend chuckled. "Christmas is not a difficult time for you, I hope?"

Grinning, Lucius shook his head. "It is not now, certainly!" His grin faded a little. "My previous plans were to stay in my own manor house for the entirety of the winter season – including Christmas."

"Your mother is not at home?"

Lucius shook his head. "No, she is not. She has chosen to take a long visit with some close friends."

"Ah."

Shrugging, Lucius surveyed the room, his smile growing. "It was somewhat difficult to accept spending so many weeks alone, but the Duke's invitation changed all of that."

Lord Renforth chuckled. "I am sure it did! I am rather surprised you arrived safely, I admit, for the roads were meant to be almost impassible in some places."

Lucius laughed wryly. "The journey here was most arduous." He rubbed one hand over his forehead, his smile dropping. "It is not one I enjoyed, but it was certainly worth it."

"I would be surprised if anyone enjoyed the journey here, I suppose." Lord Renforth grimaced. "My dear lady felt most unwell, and it is so *very* difficult to stave off the chill, no matter how many times we stopped for hot coals."

"Yes, it is very cold indeed, but I am certain here we shall have hearty fires and good cheer to warm both our bodies and our spirits." Lucius grinned, lifting his brandy in a toast to the Duke, who stood opposite them, talking to another guest. "This is an excellent idea to have such an extended house party. I think we shall be here until after Twelfth Night!"

Lord Renforth chuckled. "I do hope the Duke of Meyrick has enough good brandy for such a length of time!"

Shifting so he sat more comfortably in his chair, stretching out his legs in front of him and crossing his legs at the ankle, Lord Renforth let out a small sigh, looking rather pleased with the situation, and Lucius could only smile, quite certain the man's expression came from just how truly contented he was at present. Lucius supposed such a thing was to be expected and, no doubt, had a great deal to do with his newly married circumstances.

"I would ask you how it is to be wed, but I can tell from your expression it seems to be a very pleasant situation indeed."

Lord Renforth grinned, his eyes seeming to light as he spoke of his wife. "I have found myself in an excellent circumstance," he remarked softly. "Being wed to Lady Renforth is beyond my wildest imaginations. I knew, of course, she was a very fine lady before we wed, but I did not know how much of a gift she would be to me. I find my breath taken from me by her almost every day for she is wondrousness itself. She takes my burdens and eases them. She takes my struggles and they become lighter. I confess quite openly I find myself in love with the lady and, to my joy, she feels the very same."

Lucius' eyebrows lifted towards the ceiling. "But you never once thought to look for such an affection between you and your wife."

"Which was all the more foolish of me." Lord Renforth shook his head. "It is a situation I would recommend, for both, both Lady Renforth and I were well acquainted before our marriage, certainly, but I see now there is more to an acquaintance than simply friendship. I am certain a marriage can do well with just being kindred spirits, but to be in love with one's wife means a great deal more," he continued with a broad smile. "I would recommend such a situation to you. Find yourself a young lady you can fall deeply in love with, and thereafter, marry her. I am quite certain you will thank me for it when the time comes." Grinning, he picked up his brandy glass and held it aloft as though he were congratulating himself. "In time, you shall say to me, 'Lord Renforth, I cannot thank you enough for such kind observations as regards my present situation. I do not think I would have ever been as happy without your knowledge.' And then I shall feel a great sense of achievement and pride and *you* shall find yourself as happy as I. What do you think?"

Lucius lifted his glass and chinked it lightly against Lord Renforth's. "Perhaps you will be proven right," he suggested with a broad smile. "Although after the Season I have just endured, I believe what you have encouraged for me to pursue is still a very long way off."

At this, his friend's brows lifted high. "I had not heard."

"No, I am sure you had not heard," Lucius grinned. "After all, you were quite taken up with your own happiness, were you not?" This was said with a wink and a broad grin and immediately, Lord Renforth began to laugh, passing one hand lightly over his forehead.

"Perhaps you are a *little* correct in such things." Giving Lucius a wry smile, he put out one hand in his direction. "I am eager to listen to you now, however. Did something dreadful occur?" He chuckled quietly. "And were you the cause of it?" A glint entered his eyes, reminding Lucius of the gentleman he had once known; a gentleman who had been more of a rogue than the settled, contented fellow he was now. "Was it some dark deed you are now bearing the consequences of?"

Lucius lifted his chin. "Neither, in fact," he announced as his friend rolled his eyes, making it quite plain he did not believe him. "The truth is, I – "

Words were stolen from him as his eyes landed on a young lady who had, at that very moment, just entered the room with her mother and younger sister. A younger sister who was only just out, Lucius remembered. He could not seem to look away from her, practically staring until her eyes finally reached his. The shock he saw flaring within them filled his own heart also, for the last person he had expected to see was Miss Jane Ainsley.

"Something is wrong." His friend cleared his throat gruffly, making Lucius jerk slightly. "Who is it you are staring at, and why?"

"I am not staring," Lucius threw back quickly. "I am just a little surprised, that is all."

"Regardless of whether you are or are not staring, who is it you are looking at?" Lord Renforth demanded to know. "And please, do not pretend you are not looking in one specific direction! I know you well enough to see through such a falsehood."

The urge to repeat to his friend he had not been staring grew, but Lucius swallowed it away. "Mayhap it is providential she should appear at the very moment I am trying to tell you about what happened this Season." Muttering darkly under his breath, he settled one hand on the arm of the chair, gripping it tightly and finding it very difficult to look anywhere but her.

"Now I am all the more intrigued!"

Giving his friend a small smile, Lucius gestured to Miss Ainsley with his chin. "I am afraid the reason my summer Season was a little more difficult is standing over there - Miss Jane Ainsley."

Lord Renforth's eyes rounded as he looked over at the young lady Lucius had indicated. "A young slip of a girl like Miss Ainsley has caused you a great deal of trouble? I can hardly believe it!"

"She is not as small as you might think, for she is bold in terms of her character. There is a severity of temper also I found a little displeasing, I admit."

Although, he silently considered, *her temper had every right to flare, given the situation.*

Lord Renforth laughed. "I must say, I am very surprised indeed to hear that the young Miss Ainsley has been the cause of your distress." Turning a little more towards Lucius, he smiled expectantly. "Pray do tell me."

Lucius shrugged both shoulders. "It was a mistake, only."

Lord Renforth shook his head and chuckled, albeit a

little more darkly than before. "Understood. So it *was* your doing, after all?"

Lucius took a breath. "It was," he admitted quietly. "But it was a mistake fairly made. Perhaps I ought to have been a little more diligent before I began to pay attention to the younger sister, but –"

"The younger sister?" Lord Renforth started with such a loud exclamation that a fierce heat began to burn in Lucius' face. He dropped his head, praying Miss Ainsley would not look over at him and somehow be able to surmise what it was they were talking about.

"A little more quietly if you please."

Lord Renforth did not look happy. "You paid attention to the younger sister – the debutante?" he asked again, his words making the fire in Lucius' face grow all the hotter. Wondering if he would be able to keep any of his embarrassment to himself, Lucius shrugged.

"When I say I paid her attentions – or attempted to, at least. I hope you understand it was not with any seriousness."

Immediately Lord Renforth's face fell and seeing the graveness of his friend's expression, Lucius immediately began to protest. "I explained myself poorly. It is not what I meant."

Lord Renforth scowled, shaking his head with his expression adding weight to Lucius' already guilty heart. "I would never have gone near a debutante," he stated, as though he were attempting to protect his own honor despite the fact he had done nothing wrong. "And in fact, I did not think *you* would do such a thing either."

Nodding quickly, Lucius gestured towards his friend. "And be assured, I did not, Lord Renforth." Taking a breath, he tried to explain himself, his words toppling over each other as his friend waited expectantly. "As I have said, it was a complete misunderstanding." Lord Renforth's expression grew heavier still, and Lucius let out a groan of frustration.

"Whatever it is you are attempting to say, I do not yet understand." Lord Renforth sat a little further forward in his chair as Lucius scowled, rubbing one hand over his eyes. "Why do you not start from the beginning?"

Nodding, Lucius took in a breath, already disliking the sensation such a memory was bringing him. "There was a masquerade," he began. "I was wearing a mask that did not hide a great deal of my face – "

"Deliberately so?"

The flush that ran up Lucius' chest grew all the hotter. "Yes, deliberately so," he admitted, as Lord Renforth rolled his eyes. "I wanted to be seen. I wanted people to know who I was."

"I see."

"And after a short while, I was approached by someone I believed to be a rather... friendly lady."

Lord Renforth nodded. "Yes, and...?"

Lucius cleared his throat. "Some words were whispered into my ear by Lady Borthwick. Some particular... encouragements." His eyebrow lifted. "You know of what I am speaking, I think?"

A sudden smile crossed Lord Renforth's face. "I believe every gentleman in London knows exactly what it is you are speaking of when it comes to Lady Borthwick." The answer made Lucius chuckle, relieved his friend was willing to listen to his explanations at least.

"She was wearing a pale green gown and had a butterfly domino hiding her face. What she whispered into my ear could not be ignored. I am certain any gentleman in his right mind would not have been able to ignore it!"

Letting out a slow breath, Lord Renforth nodded his head in understanding, although he said nothing, allowing Lucius to continue.

"She bade me to come to her at a quieter part of the evening, perhaps near to the end, when everyone had enjoyed themselves – and imbibed a little more – so they might pay a little less attention as to who was present and who was not." Looking across the room towards Miss Ainsley and her sister again, he let out a heavy breath. "You can only imagine my mortification when I attempted to pull the lady away against the wall, only for Miss Ainsley to accost me and state I was laying hands on her sister!" Wincing, he shook his head. "A young lady who was only on her first Season."

Lord Renforth rolled his eyes and then let it out again with great care, his shoulders and his expression dropping.

"I understand you," he remarked quietly. "In which case, I withdraw my earlier judgment. That must have been very awkward indeed."

A dry laugh slipped from between Lucius' teeth. "Awkward is not the word I would consider using," he said with a roll of his eyes. "I did try to explain myself to Miss Ainsley, but I confess she was unwilling to listen to me."

"Which I do not think you can hold against her, either," Lord Renforth remarked. "If Miss Bettina Ainsley had been my sister, I believe I would have reacted with much the same sense of temper – perhaps even more."

Lucius grimaced. "It was a very confusing evening, I confess. Once I had apologized profusely, extricated myself from Miss Ainsley, and taken a breath, I thought to seek out Lady Borthwick, but I was not able to find her again!" It had been to his disappointment that such an offer was never given to him for the rest of the Season. Perhaps, he considered, such an opportunity would not be offered because Lady Borthwick believed he had rejected her – even though he had never had a chance to explain.

"I am certain Miss Ainsley will have forgotten about the matter," Lord Renforth said with a smile. "And if she has not, then perhaps the joy of the Christmas Season will push any dark or discounted thoughts from her mind."

Lucius opened his mouth to say he hoped so, only to notice the very lady they had been speaking of had quickly begun to make her way across the room towards them. Snapping his mouth shut, his eyes darted to Lord Renforth and then back to the lady, rather astonished she was appearing so direct.

"Good evening, Lord Northwick." The lady bobbed a curtsy and Lucius scrambled out of his chair, realizing he ought to have risen to his feet already. Miss Ainsley had not changed since their last meeting. Deep copper hair spilled from the back of her head, with a few gentle curls framing her heart-shaped face. It was her green eyes, however, that Lucius noticed the most. They were not warm but cold, flickers of steel sparkling through them. She was obviously just as displeased to see him as he was to see her.

Glancing helplessly toward Lord Renforth, Lucius quickly grasped the opportunity to find something to say rather than stand silently and stupefied. "Might I introduce the Marquess of Renforth?" he said quickly. "Lord Renforth, this is Miss Ainsley, daughter to Viscount Wilkinson."

Lord Renforth, who had risen at the same time as Lucius, bowed politely and quickly made some small conversation with the lady, which allowed Lucius to get his thoughts together. Ought he apologize once more for what had taken place? Or should he say nothing about what had happened during the summer Season?

"My father is well acquainted with the Duke of Meyrick. We were very delighted to be offered such an invitation." Finishing her answer to Lord Renforth's question, Miss Ainsley turned her attention back to Lucius. With a slight lift of her chin, she arched one eyebrow. "My younger sister is present also. I do hope you will recall my statement that you remain away from her."

Lucius inclined his head, aware of the tension growing in his stomach. "You can be assured I have no intention of coming anywhere near either yourself or your sister," he said with a small, wry smile, seeing how her cheeks colored as he included her in such a statement. "I would attempt to remind you again: it was nothing more than a misunderstanding, but I think given your present expression such an endeavor would prove to be fruitless."

Miss Ainsley curled her lip. "A *very* fruitless one indeed, Lord Northwick, since I have no belief whatsoever in a single word you say. You are well known to be something of a rogue. You may protest you believed my sister to be someone else, but such a statement does not mean I have to believe it." Raising her chin even higher, she flashed them both a sharp look before turning on her heel. Not another word was spoken, and Lucius could only watch, his hand tightly curled around his glass as she walked away.

"I do not think she likes you," Lord Renforth considered, tilting his head in Lucius' direction. "In fact, I would say Miss Ainsley is *more* than eager to stay away from you."

Lucius let out a long sigh, disliking his friend's teasing manner. "Yes, Renforth, I am well aware of her feelings, given how obvious they are."

Lord Renforth grinned, seemingly finding mirth in this rather awkward situation. "Will you do as she asks? Will you stay away from the young lady?"

Shrugging, Lucius spread his hands. "Of course, I shall," he stated plainly. "That will be no difficulty at all."

CHAPTER TWO

"It really is most frustrating." Jane stalked across the floor, flinging her gloves from her hands to her bed. "Why should he be here?"

Her sister smiled gently as she sat down on one of the chairs by the roaring fire on the other side of their bedchamber. "Because the Duke of Meyrick is allowed to invite whomever he likes to his house party, my dear sister," came the reply. "I am aware you are frustrated to see Lord Northwick present, but nothing can be done about his presence here. We must try and enjoy ourselves, regardless."

Sighing heavily, Jane rolled her eyes to herself and then shook her head, refusing to sit down in the chair opposite her sister. She was much too frustrated to relax.

"I think Lord Northwick a most disagreeable fellow — and he has a reputation for being a rogue! A gentleman such as he should not be present at a Duke's house party. I think it... unfitting." Wincing inwardly at her overeager statement, she resumed her pacing.

Bettina shook her head, letting out a quiet laugh as Jane stopped in her walking up and down the room, turning to look at her sister, a little surprised at her reaction. "Do you not think this a serious matter then? I was already quite vigilant in defending you from him before."

"As he has said – repeatedly, I believe – it was nothing more than a misunderstanding," Bettina replied quietly. "My dear sister, you do take this far too seriously. I am not at all as upset as you appear to be, yet I was the one who was almost wronged."

Jane placed her hands on her hips. "Be that as it may, a gentleman with the reputation of Lord Northwick is not a suitable gentleman for a house party such as this, not when there are so very many eligible young ladies present. What happens if he should try to shower his attentions upon one of them when they do not wish it?"

Her sister pinched the bridge of her nose, shaking her head gently. Jane dropped her shoulders as her hands fell to her sides, afraid she was becoming a little too dramatic, but the concern she had felt for her younger sister had been insurmountable, still flashing through her despite the fact the London Season was, by now, some months ago back.

"I think you are being a little too unfair to Lord Northwick."

Jane said nothing, blowing air out through her nose as she waited for her sister to explain further.

"Lord Northwick thought I was someone else," Bettina continued quietly, although her gaze was steady and firm. "I do not think he had any thoughts towards garnering affections from a young lady such as myself. You did not tell me which lady it was he was expecting to pull away into the shadows, but I am sure she was no debutante! In fact, I think the reason you have not told me her name is because you do not wish me to know about her." Her smile grew. "Might I be correct?"

Jane turned her head away, refusing to speak to her sister any longer about the matter. The truth was, of course, she was resisting the urge to tell her sister all about Lady Borthwick, precisely because the lady was so well known amongst London society that it would be impossible to keep any of the rumors about her character and her particular acquaintances away from Bettina's ears. The less her sister knew about the darker sides of society, the better.

"Jane?"

She glanced back over her shoulder. "I am your elder sister. It is my job, therefore, to protect you as best I can."

"Which you know I appreciate, but I am afraid you cannot protect me from everything," her sister replied. "You cannot protect me, for example, from knowing about Lady Borthwick! I know she is a widowed lady who is eager for the company of gentlemen. I have heard she looks through all of society, decides which gentlemen she wants for herself, and then begins to make her attempts. I am also well aware that the gentleman of society know of this reputation she carries and are eager to make her one of their own conquests."

Jane's eyes flared, but Bettina only laughed aloud at her horrified look. "Come now, Jane," she finished, settling her hands in her lap. "You must realize I am not about to be kept from everything. I may only have had my debut in the summer, but I was thrust into the middle of London society and therefore know almost everything there is to know – dark or otherwise, pleasant or distasteful. I am afraid I have a good many friends who are eager to tell me everything I wish – and even do not wish – to know."

Jane's shoulders dropped, her spirits sinking. With a heavy sigh, she gave up her pacing, coming to sit opposite her sister instead. "I see." She shook her head. "You think me ridiculous, perhaps, for attempting to keep you from such objectionable things when I myself have only just had my second Season." Her wry expression seemed to make her sister laugh again, although Jane found nothing mirthful in the entire situation.

"I do not think you foolish. I think you kind."

Reaching across and bending forward in her chair, Bettina pressed Jane's hand. "But I would ask you not to be too harsh in your demeanor when it comes to Lord North-wick. You have always been quite determined to believe he did such a thing purposefully, that he ought to have known better or have been much more careful." A sigh left her as she looked directly back at Jane, her hands returning to clasp together in her lap as she sat back in her chair. "I will not pretend the latter is not true. Yes, he should have been a good deal more careful. He was not and, because of his care-lessness, a mistake was made."

"A *severe* mistake."

Hearing the darkness in her voice and aware she might sound as though she were scolding Bettina, Jane looked away just as her sister sighed gently. It took some moments for Jane to be willing to speak, but when she did, her voice was heavy. "Very well, you may be right. I *am* holding some-thing of a grudge against Lord Northwick. He may have given us excuses, but I do not believe them. I know you do but I simply cannot. Lord Northwick is known to be some-thing of a rogue – although not a bad one, of course."

Bettina held out both hands to her sides. "I cannot really believe a gentleman such as he would deliberately tug a debutante away from her mother and sister in the middle of a masquerade ball. A gentleman who, I might add, I was not even introduced to! That would be foolishness itself, my dear sister, for he could have severely damaged his reputation, even if he is considered something of a rogue. There would have been a scandal if he had been caught. I think if you were to consider matters a little more, you might realize he *is* speaking the truth." Lifting her shoulders, she shrugged. "He thought I was someone else. There is nothing more to it."

Taking a deep breath. Jane considered this for some minutes. They had barely spoken of Lord Northwick since the unfortunate evening in London- and for good reason. There had been much else to discuss, including the gentlemen who had shown an interest in both Bettina and some also showing an interest in Jane herself. There was no immediate concern, however, over Jane's lack of courtship – not as yet. Come next Season, she would *have* to find a match. But whether or not such a thing would happen, she could not say, although she desperately wished for it to be so. To be invited to the Duke's house party, however, was a boon for her, and as she considered this, Jane silently began to realize she should not allow Lord Northwick's presence to damage this opportunity.

"You are right." Admitting such a thing was not at all painful, although Bettina's eyebrows lifted in evident surprise. "We should not judge him too harshly. If he did make such a mistake, then it was foolish indeed. But if he speaks the truth, then we – or, in fact, I – need to have no concern over his behavior towards you, or what may occur at this house party."

Bettina's eyebrows remained lifted. "Good gracious. I do hope you have had no concerns about *my* behavior! I have no intention of going anywhere near him, if that is what you are worried about." Catching the slight flicker of concern in her sister's eyes, Jane was quick to reassure her.

"No, I do not consider myself at all worried about you,"

she answered quickly. "In fact, I would not recommend going to speak with Lord Northwick – for I myself had to do so and found it to be very awkward indeed!"

Bettina laughed, her green eyes – so similar to Jane's – sparkling. "I understand." With a wry smile, she lifted both shoulders gently. "Then let us both be genteel and polite towards him, but certainly not overly friendly," she continued as Jane nodded her agreement. "It will be for the best... for *all* of us."

"DID YOU HEAR?" Jane and her sister sat with the other ladies in the drawing room, having finished what had been a magnificent dinner. Tea had been served,and they were all enjoying a pleasant cup as they waited for the gentlemen to join them. "There is to be a bullet cake one evening!"

"A bullet cake?" Jane repeated, her stomach immediately dropping low. "Goodness, I do not think I should want to take part in such a game."

"Oh, but you must!" Bettina exclaimed at once. "My dear sister, we are at the Duke's Christmas house party! It is meant to be exciting – but what fun are we to have if you do not take part in any of the games?"

Jane bit her lip, seeing what her sister meant, but finding herself struggling with the idea, nonetheless. She did not want to take part in a bullet cake, for then she might find herself with a face full of flour, and to appear so would be most embarrassing indeed.

The door opened and the gentlemen walked in before they could say anything further about such a game, and Jane was left to consider exactly what games were to be played this particular evening, wondering if she might find a way to excuse herself without her appearing to be either miserable or rude.

"We are to play a game this evening!" Lady Meyrick clapped her hands, catching everyone's attention as the gentlemen all found a seat. Some had very broad smiles on their faces, which, no doubt, was an effect of the port they had enjoyed after dinner.

"It is a very simple game." Lady Meyrick continued. "I am sure we shall all enjoy it since there are so many of us!"

Reminding herself not to be too serious about such things, Jane took in a breath and settled back into her chair a little. It would be foolish of her to give an impression of a severe aversion to such things, for if one could not have fun at the Christmas party, then when could one?

"I will explain the rules." The Duke of Meyrick rose to his feet and began to tell them all what would occur – and Jane realized just how simple a game it truly was. One person would be blindfolded while another was sent outside the room. Everyone remaining would move about to a different place within the room, with some hiding in the shadows or standing in awkward places to make it more difficult. Thereafter, the person blindfolded would be unmasked and given three opportunities to state which person was absent. The guesses had to be offered with some haste, for if anyone should take too long, then they would have to take a forfeit, regardless! Should they manage to guess correctly, then the person standing outside of the room would be the one blindfolded. If they did not guess correctly, however, then a forfeit would be undertaken.

"A forfeit?" her sister whispered, as Jane winced. "Does she mean....?"

As Lady Meyrick gestured to the fire, which was still burning merrily, Jane let out a small sigh. "Some coal will be taken from it, or some ash from the grate beneath. It will be used to smudge the faces of those who had guessed incorrectly."

Bettina took in a breath. "Goodness."

"Although it may be you wish to offer *another* forfeit," Lady Meyrick finished with a wiggle of her eyebrows, which made some gentleman chortle and many a young lady blush. Jane looked away, finding it very difficult indeed to look at anyone in particular, afraid they would see the color in her face. What was it she would take if she were offered the choice to pick between the two? Would she offer some trinket to a gentleman, knowing he would have every right to ask her for whatever he wished when he returned it to her? Or would she have her face blackened with coal dust instead? Jane simply could not determine which one was more preferable. Her fingers twisted together in her lap, tension billowing like a sail. Perhaps she would neither be chosen nor would fail, in which case no forfeit would be required of her. Such an outcome was the only one that would bring her any relief.

"Now you must look around the room." Lady Meyrick continued as the game began. "See how there are many little shadowy places, many corners and things which you might wish to hide behind, so long as you are still able to be seen by the person who is blindfolded when the time comes, then all will be well. You may hide some of yourself, but not all of yourself, if you understand my meaning!"

"I believe we all fully understand." Lord Stone chuckled, making some in the room laugh. "Shall I be the first to step forward and take part? I assume you have the blindfold, Lady Meyrick?"

Everyone else in the room clapped and laughed as the game began, but Jane could only feel a sense of dread beginning to flood her. She would much prefer a game where there were no forfeits at all, where they might play with graciousness and calmness rather than these frankly overt exchanges. One glance at her sister told her, however, she was the only one who felt this way, for almost everybody else in the room had either a broad smile on their face or light in their eyes, showing they appeared to be enjoying every moment. With a deep breath, Jane closed her eyes for a moment, telling herself she had to find a little merriment somewhere within herself. She was not that way inclined, of course, being a good deal more studious and sensible than her sister, but perhaps this house party was a time and an opportunity for her to shake it off a little, to embrace the laughter and the Christmas time. Regardless, she was not entirely convinced she would enjoy it.

CHAPTER THREE

"I do confess I am finding this game a little tedious."

Whether or not Lady Meyrick overheard his muttered remark to Lord Stone, Lucius did not know, but at that very moment, she whirled around and pointed one finger at him.

"This time we shall have *two* absent from the room!" she exclaimed, bringing a murmur from some of the other guests. "So you see, Lord Winchester, you shall have to recall two people rather than one."

"I confess it seems a little unfair." Lord Winchester folded his arms across his chest and grinned, despite his covered eyes, making everyone laugh. "But very well, I shall do as you have bade me, since you are the lady of the house."

Lucius dutifully made his way as quietly as he could to step out of the room, pushing the door soundlessly. Leaning against the wall, he let out a long and heavy sigh. To him, certainly, he had been playing this game for far too long. His sigh snaked down the hallway as he closed his eyes. Whatever other entertainment Lady Meyrick or the Duke himself had planned, Lucius hoped it would come very soon.... or that they would play some other game entirely.

"Perhaps I am just in a disagreeable mood, given I have not been able to gain a forfeit from anyone," he muttered, a little darkly. Forfeits were the best part of Christmas parties, for they meant trinkets and trinkets meant kisses, and he could easily be cheered by a swift press of a young lady's lips against his! Thus far, however, he had not been able to gain even a single one.

The door opened again, but Lucius did not even turn his head, such was his mood. It was only when a soft exclamation left the lady's lips that he finally looked over, quickly then pushing himself away from the wall as he realized he stood in the presence of Miss Ainsley.

"I can assure you, this was not done purposefully," he said quickly, only for Miss Ainsley to send him one short, quick glance.

"Of course it was not done purposefully." Turning a little away from him, Miss Ainsley folded her arms across her chest. "Lady Meyrick has now decided to choose two people per turn and given both you and I have not yet had opportunity to step out of the room, I can see it was done purely by chance." She did not say another word, although Lucius did note the slight color in her cheeks. Becoming a little frustrated himself at the sharpness she had used in speaking with him, he found himself moving closer to her, suddenly speaking in a harsher tone.

"I am aware we have already spoken, Miss Ainsley, but I should like to know when this particular coldness you push towards me will be at an end. Are we to be like this for the entirety of the house party, or might we, at the very least, attempt to be amiable?" The moment his words died away, Lucius winced. He had not spoken well, he realized.

He had been a little too harsh rather than being calm and gentle in his words. But then again, he reasoned silently, Miss Ainsley had shown him no such kindness.

"I think I have good reason for behaving as I do, Lord Northwick," Miss Ainsley told him, her arms still folded tight and her eyes still fixed on his. "My sister has also attempted to tell me it was nothing more than a misunderstanding, but I myself I am not sure. You are known to be a bit of a rogue. You say you would not have touched a debutante, but again, I cannot trust your words to be true."

"That may be, but there are things you could do to prove to yourself what I say is true." Finding himself suddenly rather eager for Miss Ainsley to see the truth of his words, Lucius came a little closer to her. "You might speak to some of my friends who are present here at this house party – Lord Renforth, for example, will promise you I am not a gentleman who would *ever* go near a debutante. Perhaps such a thing will be enough to convince you I am not the fellow you think me."

Miss Ainsley hesitated, bit her lip, and then, much to Lucius' surprise, dropped her hands to her side, shook her head, and let out a heavy sigh. It took some moments for her to explain herself, however, and Lucius simply stood there, watching her change in expression.

"I am sorry."

Lucius' eyes flared in surprise, and he found himself moving back a little, inwardly realizing just how intimidating he might have appeared in standing so close, particularly when they were alone.

"I should not be holding a grudge." This was said with a tight smile and eyes that flicked in his direction before quickly traveling away again. "You say it was a mistake – a misunderstanding. I confess I am not inclined to believe you, but it does not mean I should continue to treat you in this cold and somewhat condescending manner." With a small shrug, she looked away. "We will not be friends, Lord Northwick, not by any means, but I can at least be a little more... civil." Taking another breath, she let it out slowly. "From this moment on, I intend to do so."

Such an admission gave Lucius a chance to see the young lady as he had never seen her before. He allowed himself to look at her for a little longer than he might otherwise have permitted himself, taking her in, seeing just how her expression changed, her demeanor altered. Now, however, she did not appear to be so resistant to his company, something changed within him also as he looked into her face, their eyes meeting and melding for a few long moments. Blinking rapidly. Lucius shook his head, and opened his mouth to say something more – just as the door was flung open and Lady Meyrick beckoned them both back inside.

"Lord Winchester has only guessed one of you correctly." Her smile grew as she looked toward Miss Ainsley. "You are quite safe, dear lady." With a laugh, she turned back towards Lucius, who found himself groaning gently, his shoulders dropping as he attempted to smile. "Alas, you, Lord Northwick, do not have such luck! It is now your turn to be blindfolded."

Lucius nodded, albeit rather unwillingly. "Very well," he agreed, throwing a quick glance towards Miss Ainsley. She, however, had already turned her head away and was making her way back towards the door without giving him so much as a backward glance. For whatever reason, Lucius found her seeming lack of interest incredibly frustrating but there was no time to linger on such feelings for he was then swiftly taken back into the drawing room. Led by Lady

Meyrick, who then proceeded to blindfold him as the room was filled with giggles and laughter, Lucius merely stood there, concentrating on the sound of his breath rather than on the joviality around him. For whatever reason, his mind was fixed not on the game but solely Miss Ainsley. Even when the blindfold was taken off, he could see none but her. She was sitting quietly on one of the couches, looking back at him as though she wanted him to see how obvious she was and did not want his gaze to linger. Lucius set his jaw as he forced his gaze elsewhere, but he could not seem to concentrate on any of the other faces he saw. No doubt Miss Ainsley's frustrating behavior was the reason for him being unable to forget about her. There were a few giggles and plenty of laughter, but Lucius himself did not so much as break into a smile. Eventually he guessed one name and then a second, without having any real idea about whether or not these people were present in the room. Even though it was entirely foolish of him to do so, he named Miss Ainsley as his third guess, all the while looking directly back at her. It was as though something within him wanted to speak her name aloud.

At this, Lady Meyrick laughed merrily and set one hand on his shoulder. "You are quite correct, Lord Northwick!"

Blinking in surprise, Lucius turned his head around, not certain as to what Lady Meyrick meant. Miss Ainsley was present. She was sitting on the coach directly opposite him. What, then, could Lady Meyrick mean?

With a flash of recognition, Lucius' eyes flared – just as Lady Meyrick spoke.

"You may come in now, Miss Ainsley."

It was not the elder Miss Ainsley who was absent, but rather the younger. His face flushed as he glanced towards the elder Miss Ainsley, seeing her eyes narrow slightly.

What could he say? Yet again, this was nothing more than another coincidence, something which had happened without his intention or knowledge. And yet now, the younger Miss Ainsley would have to give him one of her trinkets by way of a forfeit – and Lucius could see in the elder Miss Ainsley's eyes just how it upset her.

"Alas, Miss Ainsley, you have been discovered." Lady Meyrick laughed, shaking her head. "I am afraid when one has such beauty as you do, it is almost impossible for the gentlemen in this room to forget you." Beckoning the young lady forward, Lady Meyrick chuckled again. "I am afraid she must offer Lord Northwick a forfeit. You have a choice now, Miss Ainsley! Either you offer Lord Northwick a trinket and, in time, he can come to take your forfeit, or shall you have your face smudged with dust?"

Feeling vastly uncomfortable, Lucius glanced from one Miss Ainsley to the other. Everyone else appeared to be enjoying the moment as much as they had done with the other gentlemen and ladies who are required to pay a forfeit, but this situation unsettled him greatly. Mayhap, he considered, it came from the fact the elder Miss Ainsley was continuing to glare at him as though he had done such a thing intentionally.

"I offer you a forfeit." Miss Ainsley pulled something from her reticule and handed it to him with a smile – a smile Lucius did not return. He took it from the young lady, and thereafter, turned quickly back towards his seat, dragging his gaze away from Miss Ainsley. The game continued as Lucius merely sat forward in his seat, his hands twirling the small silver hairpin Miss Bettina Ainsley had given to him. The fact he had previously been a little upset over gaining not even a single forfeit now seemed incredibly foolish, and Lucius found himself wishing he had never yearned for such a thing.... or that the forfeit had been from anyone other than Miss Bettina Ainsley.

"Although I am just as relieved I did not take it from Miss Jane Ainsley." Muttering to himself, a small smile touched his lips. He would return the trinket it Miss Bettina Ainsley with only a small forfeit required – perhaps a kiss to the back of her hand or some other small gesture – and perhaps also in the presence of Miss Jane Ainsley. In doing it in such a way, then neither of them could complain for, firstly, he would have done as he ought, and secondly, he would not have done too much. Hopefully, it would bring the matter to an end and Miss Jane Ainsley would stop throwing daggers directly at him in her gaze. Averting his gaze, Lucius considered for a moment. Mayhap he might have to consider stepping aside from any game where the younger Miss Ainsley was to be a part of his group for he could not permit such a thing to happen again! Allowing his gaze to flick to Miss Jane Ainsley's face once more, he caught the narrowing of her gaze and, with a sigh, averted his gaze entirely.

Things were not about to become any simpler between him and the two sisters, no matter how much he wished it.

It was some time after the ladies retired that Lucius found himself fatigued enough to make his way to bed. The evening had, on the whole, been a pleasant one, albeit filled with the ongoing, fierce glances Miss Ainsley had sent him! The younger sister, however, had not appeared to be at all upset by what had occurred, clearly accepting it to all be part of the game – and, in fact, had smiled at him when he had looked over at her. Lucius considered she was a rather pleasant young woman and, in comparing her to her elder sister, found Miss Jane Ainsley severely lacking. Why could she not see it had been a mistake the night of the masquerade ball? Why was she so determined to think ill of him? What he had said by way of explanation was the truth. Why did she feel the need to pore over his words and search his expression? Wandering towards his room, Lucius found his thoughts holding fast to Miss Jane Ainsley, and it was with a great effort he turned them elsewhere.

So far, he was enjoying the house party on the whole, appreciating the opportunity to get to know some new acquaintances as well as deepen friendships with current acquaintances. This was one of the longest house parties he had ever attended, for it would take them right through Christmas and into the early days of January. However, he was rather pleased to be doing so, for the fact was Lucius would have otherwise been entirely alone. Yes, he had a brother, for what esteemed family did not have an heir and a spare? But his brother was gone to the continent, inspecting their late father's holdings and Lucius did not expect him back for another twelve months and with his mother visiting friends, there was no one else for Lucius to spend such a time as this with. Thus, when the invitation had come, he had accepted it almost at the very same moment he had received it, writing a letter immediately and sending it back without a second of hesitation. He had accepted the Duke's invitation with warmest regards, he recalled. Thus, just because Miss Ainsley was present, did not mean he had to find it in any way displeasing.

With a sigh that told him he knew all too well he was thinking of Miss Jane Ainsley yet again, Lucius reached his bedchamber, opened the door, and stepped inside. The room was warm, for a fire had been kept lit for him – there was nothing to be spared for the guests, it seemed – and he was sure there would have been a warming pan filled with hot charcoal and ashes run around under the covers until just a few moments before he had arrived. Given the lateness of the hour, he had informed his valet he would put himself to bed and did not require his services further but now that it came to it, Lucius found himself a little irritated he had done so, for he could easily have used the fellow's help, given how fatigued he was.

He stopped suddenly. There was something placed upon his dressing table – a small folded note, tied with a ribbon. He looked at it for a long moment before he continued to approach, as though it might jump out to frighten him in some way. Something ran through his frame, flooding him with concern over what such a note could be. To be sealed with a ribbon, to his mind, meant it had been written by the hand of a lady. Starting forward, Lucius reached for the note, letting the ribbon fall away as he held it up. A gentle hint of lavender came towards him and immediately, something twisted in his gut. He had no doubt now that someone had written him a letter – and that someone was certainly a lady.

Aware his reputation had a touch of the rogue about it, Lucius unfolded the note quickly and let his eyes fall upon the few lines.

'I have been watching you, Lord Northwick. You are the most handsome of gentlemen. I hope we might further our acquaintance to a fresh warmth during this house party. Yours.'

Nothing more was said in the note, nothing to tell him who had written it, and yet excitement poured into him, which quickly roared into a flaming fire. Taking the note, he sat down on the bed once more, silently thinking over each and every lady present at the house party. One of them had written to him. One of them had to set their expectations upon him, although what exactly it was they were looking for he could not say. Throwing one hand over his eyes, Lucius began again, murmuring each lady's name as he went. It seemed very strange to him once he reached the end, for many of them were debutantes or as yet unwed young ladies present with their parents and surely would not dare do such a thing, whereas everyone else was either engaged or wed.

"I am not so much a rogue as that," he stated aloud to himself. Whoever this was, they must not be fully aware of his reputation. Yes, there was a hint of the rogue in him, but he never once dallied with a debutante or with a married lady. A kiss stolen here or there, a gentle glance, some teasing and flirtation was all he would ever do – and only with those he deemed suitable.

Shaking his head, he folded up the note again and then rose at his feet, wandering towards the fire. Hesitating, he held it above the flames, thinking to himself he would throw it in there and allow it to be burnt to ash.

After a moment, however, he folded it up again and, walking across the room, placed it in the top drawer of his dresser. A scent of lavender lingered there for a few moments more, but Lucius refused to allow his mind to contemplate the question of who had sent it any longer. Instead, he began to prepare himself for bed, quite eager now to lose himself in the unconsciousness of sleep. Such questions could wait until the morrow.

CHAPTER FOUR

"My dear Miss Ainsley, I am very pleased to see you this morning. You are as early as I am, I think."

Jane nodded quickly, aware of the gentle grumbling in her stomach. "I am not one inclined to linger in bed." She smiled at Lady Farquhar, who inclined her head back in return, as though agreeing with her.

The truth was, Jane had struggled to stay asleep, given that her mind had been filled with none other than Lord Northwick. She had been telling herself repeatedly that what he had done in taking a forfeit from her sister could have not been planned in any way. Yet part of her wanted to believe that somehow he had used Lady Meyrick to gain access to her sister. For now, Bettina had been forced to give Lord Northwick a trinket, and the trinket could be used to gain anything from a dance to a kiss. What was it he had wanted? To show Jane he could get whatever he wished from whomever he wished, regardless of her attempts to stop him? She had not said anything to her sister, of course, for no doubt, Bettina would roll her eyes and tell her she was being quite ridiculous, which Jane was, truthfully, beginning to believe. But for whatever reason, the smile on Lord Northwick's face when he had taken Bettina's hair pin was one she had not been able to remove from her mind, and thus, she had found herself awake much too early.... to her own frustration also.

"I did hear Lady Borthwick arrived late last evening. Are you acquainted with her?"

Jane's stomach clenched immediately at the sound of Lady Borthwick's name. *That* was the lady Lord Northwick had supposedly been seeking out on the night of the masquerade ball, when he had grabbed her sister instead.

"No, I confess I am not." Silently praying that someone else would soon come to join them at the dining table, she chose some items from the breakfast table for her plate. "I know very little of her, in fact."

"Well, I am sure you will become acquainted with her very soon. She is to join us for breakfast, so long as she is not too fatigued from her journey." Lady Farquhar smiled, her eyes drifting towards the door at the other end of the room as though she expected Lady Borthwick to step in at any moment. "She and I have been great friends for many a year. Her situation is so very sad. She lost her husband only a few years after they wed."

"Does she have any children?"

Lady Farquhar beamed. "Oh yes, she does. She gave her husband the heir before he so tragically died. A lovely boy, I must say. Of course, he is at Eton now."

"His presence must be some comfort at least." Giving the lady a small smile, Jane silently prayed the conversation would be brought to an end as quickly as it could, so she might think of something other than Lady Borthwick. It was clear Lady Borthwick was now able to live in comfort and contentment, given the fact her son was now the new Lord Borthwick. It also meant she could have as many close companions as she wished, but without any specific requirement for her to wed. The more she thought of it, the less Jane wanted to continue the conversation. Much to her relief, the door opened. She looked up eagerly, believing her prayers were answered, only for her hopes to immediately sink back down. With what was a small, slightly uncomfortable looking smile and eyes darted about the room rather than linger on either on her or Lady Farquhar's face, Lord Northwick came to join them.

"Good morning." His throat was a little gruff as he inclined his head. Fair hair fell forward across his forehead only to be swept back, his angular face a little sharper with a tight expression rather than a smile. His hazel eyes were dark as he glanced around the room, lingering on Jane for only a moment.

"Good morning!" Lady Farquhar exclaimed with great enthusiasm as Jane murmured something vague thereafter. "The rest of our company are, I fear, still abed. I do not think we will have their company for some time yet." She sounded quite delighted that the three of them should be alone together, whereas Jane found herself wincing at the idea.

Lord Northwick returned Lady Farquhar's smile, but it cleared shortly thereafter. "I do hope you both slept well?"

Jane gave him a small nod, choosing not to say anything while, thankfully, Lady Farquhar appeared quite eager to have the conversation all to herself. She was speaking at great length about the difficulties she had in sleep in her later years and warned Jane directly about these things, stating they would come upon her at some point in her life. She then went on to narrate the plethora of remedies she had tried – although not all of them were considered help-ful. All in all, she spoke without stopping for some minutes and Jane found herself willing her to continue on even a little more.

The door opened again, and as Jane took a bite of toast, her eyes caught a lady stepping through the door. It was someone she had never seen before, for as yet, she had not been present at the Duke's house party. It took her only a moment of clarity to realize this must be none other than Lady Borthwick – and with a quick breath, her gaze imme-diately went to Lord Northwick.

"Ah, good morning! We have been waiting for your arrival."

It came as no surprise to Jane that Lady Farquhar was instantly ready with her greeting. Jane nodded her welcome, just as Lord Northwick's head swiveled to his right. He seemed to start with surprise, his fingers clutching the edge of the table, only for him to rise swiftly as he turned towards the lady.

"I did not realize you would be present, Lady Borth-wick," Lord Northwick murmured, as Lady Borthwick directed her smile toward him.

"I was very glad to be invited." Approaching the table, Lady Borthwick drew closer to Lord Northwick. "My son is gone to his uncle's for the festive season." A small sigh escaped her as her smile began to fall away. "It is the one thing my late husband's brother insists on, and I do not have the heart to refuse. My son does so very much love his uncle and I am aware that the connection is good for the both of them. Nonetheless, I find that I am a little lonely without him, for the older he becomes, the less time I have to spend with him!" A small sigh escaped her. "It is for his good, I suppose."

Lady Farquhar immediately held out the hand towards Lady Borthwick, and after a moment she took it, with a slight glistening about her clear blue eyes. Jane found herself rather surprised at this, for she did not think a lady of quality such as Lady Borthwick would express her emotions so very easily and so openly, given she was in mixed company – some whom she knew and some she did not. Indeed, this also did not fit with the conniving, selfish creature Jane had heard so much about.

"You will see him before he returns to Eton, I hope?" Lord Northwick asked, as Jane stirred her tea carefully, not wanting to interrupt the conversation.

Lady Borthwick blinked rapidly, her faint smile growing a little. "Yes, for a short while at least. I do miss him very much, but he is being taught to grow into such a fine gentleman, so I cannot complain. He will require a great deal of tutelage, since his father is... no longer present to teach him such things."

Something tore in Jane's heart and she found herself murmuring something she hoped would be comforting to the lady. Lady Borthwick then turned her gaze towards Jane, and on seeing this, Lady Farquhar quickly made the introductions. Jane smiled, rose, dropped into a curtsy, and then sat back down, allowing the conversation to continue on with her input – although Lord Northwick was the one who spoke first.

"Do you intend to stay for the entirety of the house party, Lady Borthwick?"

There was something in his voice Jane had never heard before - a lightness, perhaps? Undoubtedly something that spoke of pleasure and delight. Her stomach twisted hard and she dropped her eyes to the floor, suddenly finding herself completely disinterested in her food although she could not give any explanation as to why.

"I have every intention of staying for as long as the house party continues." Lady Borthwick answered with a warm smile in Lord Northwick's direction. "And you, Lord Northwick. Do you have any intention of staying here for the duration, or shall you take your leave a little earlier?"

Lord Northwick grinned. "I have every plan to stay, Lady Borthwick," he answered, the warmth in his voice growing with every word. "And with fine company such as yourself, I am sure this house party will be all the more pleasurable."

Without explanation, a flush begun began to rise up Jane's neck, and the heat continued to rise to the very top of her head. She could not say where it had come from nor why it continued to burn through to her very soul, but yet there it still remained. Could it be she was jealous? Jealous that Lord Northwick seemed so pleased to be in Lady Borthwick's company, but not her own? Such a notion would make very little sense, however, for she had no desire to be in Lord Northwick's company, nor did she want him to delight in her presence.

"We have been playing many a parlor game," Lady Farquhar informed her. "There have been some forfeits given already!"

"Is that so?" Lady Borthwick laughed, her eyes suddenly sparkling as Jane continued to watch the interplay, both frustrated and intrigued in the very same measure. "I am sorry I have been absent from these games!"

"It is all quite by chance, of course, as to who one receives a forfeit from." There was a new firmness to Lord Northwick's tone, forcing her gaze towards him. "Lady Meyrick was organizing a game only last evening. By the end of the night, I received not one, but *two* forfeits, although I was very fortunate indeed not to have my face dusted with coal dust!"

A ring of laughter ran around the table and Jane demanded her lips curve into a smile, even though she had no inclination to do so. Such remarks had been for her; she was sure of it. Lord Northwick was attempting to make it quite clear he had done nothing by which to garner a forfeit from her sister. Jane dropped her eyes back to the table, a small sense of embarrassment rising. Despite what she had said to him last evening, the truth was, she did not particularly like the gentleman, and yet, for whatever reason, found herself considering him all the more. Despite the fact she had never said anything to him directly, Lord Northwick was making it quite clear he had not done a single thing to encourage Lady Meyrick into giving him a hint as to who had gone out of the room.

"It is all a game of chance, is it not?" she said, lifting her head and looking directly at Lady Borthwick. Now was the time to speak as directly as she could, to show she could be gracious enough to accept she had been wrong to even *think* he had done such a thing. Pressing her lips together, she looked toward Lord Northwick.

The gentleman's eyes twinkled, a small smile lifting his mouth, but it was Lady Borthwick who spoke.

"But you see, Miss Ainsley, in circumstances such as these and with these sorts of parlor games, there is always trickery and tomfoolery afoot! You may not believe it and mayhap, within the first few games such a thing does not take place, but I can assure you that come the end of the first sennight, there will be gentlemen whispering into Lady Meyrick's ear and she, of course, will be delighted to oblige."

Concern immediately began to fling itself into Jane's mind. "What do you mean?"

This time, both Lady Farquhar and Lady Borthwick shared a look, laughing softly as they did so.

"Why, my dear Miss Ainsley, there are, at present, *many* merry gentlemen eager to steal a kiss from a specific young lady," Lady Farquhar explained, her eyes twinkling. "And this is the way to get such a thing! It is mayhap a little underhanded but at such times as this, it is almost expected. You may find yourself the interest of a particular gentleman, finding he has swapped forfeits with another gentleman, simply so he might be in your company a little more."

A blush mounted on Jane's face and she could not, for whatever reason, seem to look in Lord Northwick's direction

"I can assure you, however, not all gentlemen will behave in such a way," she heard Lord Northwick say, but his words only brought fresh laughter from the two other ladies.

"You are attempting to make out that you are *quite* the honorable gentleman, are you not?" Lady Borthwick shook her head, reaching across the table and pressing Lord Northwick's arm. "Very well. Let us pretend for the moment you *are* such a gentleman, given that Miss Ainsley is present."

Pushing herself out of her chair with a sudden urgency, no longer able to listen to the conversation, no longer willing to hear another word, Jane hurried to the door. Yes, she had known Lord Northwick had a reputation – although it was certainly not as scandalous as many of the gentlemen in London – but for whatever reason, hearing this from these two ladies seemed to be more than she could bear. "Excuse me. I think I should go to make certain my sister has risen from her bed. I should not like her to miss this morning's activities."

Lady Borthwick and Lady Farquhar did not seem to notice her concern, for the latter gave her a wave, but continued to talk to Lady Borthwick. Scurrying from the room and closing the door behind her, Jane took a breath before beginning to walk down the hallway.

Only for someone to call her name.

Glancing over her shoulder, she was astonished to see none other than Lord Northwick following after her.

"Miss Ainsley." Lord Northwick put out one hand, then pulled it back sharply. "I wanted to assure you that, despite what was said by Lady Borthwick, I have never been a gentleman who has ever taken advantage of a young lady. I have never ruined a reputation, nor caused a scandal, I can assure you."

Jane considered this, looking into the depths of his eyes and finding something within her beginning to grow into a slow-burning fire, instead of the ice she usually felt forming around her heart whenever she spoke with him.

"I see." She did not say whether or not she believed him and watched as Lord Northwick's shoulders slumped a little.

"If you wish it, you may take your sister's forfeit for yourself." Lifting his head so his eyes looked straight into hers, as if he wanted to prove to her he meant every word simply by such a severe look, he put out both hands. "If it would make you feel more at ease, then I would be glad to do so. That way, you will have no lingering concern. Otherwise, I can assure you I will ask her for nothing of any seriousness."

"You would give me my sister's hairpin?" Her heart

quickened a little in surprise. "And you would do that only to prove yourself to me?"

Lord Northwick held her gaze for a long moment as something warm pooled in her stomach, speaking of relief and even happiness. She considered him for a few moments. Would she accept her sister's trinket from Lord Northwick, knowing full well Bettina herself would be very frustrated with her for doing so? But perhaps she would be protecting her, would she not?

"Miss Ainsley?"

After some moments, Jane lifted her chin a little and cleared her throat. Lord Northwick's eyes were searching hers, as though he were opening himself up, willing her to look into the depths of his soul and find he was not wanting as she believed him to be.

"I should not like my sister to be irritated with me." Taking a breath, she lifted one shoulder lightly. "Truthfully, I would have liked to accept your offer, but I believe Bettina would be a little angry with me if I did as you offer, although I shall hold you to your word that you will do nothing other than press a kiss to the back of her hand or take a dance you favor."

"But of course." Lord Northwick nodded firmly, and much to Jane's astonishment, reached out one hand to touch her hand. He took it for a moment, looking back into her face, and then, without another word, stepped back and began to walk away. The touch of his fingers against her own sent sparks zipping up her arm, her heart tumbling over itself as she found herself watching after him. Why she could not pull her eyes away and resume her own walk down the hallway, Jane did not understand, but there was something about Lord Northwick that seemed to grasp her attention – to the point that she could do nothing else. Her eyes held to the back of him as he made his way into the dining room without so much as a glance over his shoulder – and for whatever reason, Jane found it a little frustrating. There was no reason as to why she should feel such a way, however, and silently berating herself, Jane turned and walked with quick strides along the hallway.

"It is foolishness to let my thoughts linger on him." Muttering quietly to herself, Jane walked towards her bedchamber, trying to set aside the smile she had seen on Lord Northwick's face when he had spoken with Lady Borthwick, a smile that had spoken of a previous acquaintance. Now, however, it meant she had been wrong about what had taken place the night of the masquerade ball. What she could not seem to understand, however, was why her heart disliked seeing such a smile on his face. She did not like Lord Northwick, so why should she care if he smiled so warmly at anyone else? It was naught more than foolishness, she told herself, but regardless, the awareness continued to linger. It was only when she found her sister – who *had*, in fact, risen from her bed – and began a conversation with her that she was finally able to push Lord Northwick from her thoughts... and if she did not think of him again, Jane would be very pleased indeed.

CHAPTER FIVE

*I*t must *be from Lady Borthwick.*

Smiling at the particular lady across the room, Lucius let himself think of all that might take place, should he accept Lady Borthwick's offer of warming their acquaintance a little more, as the note had suggested. Lady Borthwick was a most beautiful widowed lady, but she had never offered her acquaintance to Lucius before – not since the night of the masquerade ball. Now, it was practically being handed to him and Lucius was not about to refuse it, although why his gaze was pulling itself towards Miss Ainsley, he could not understand. It was a little frustrating, in fact, to find himself looking over at the young lady rather than toward Lady Borthwick.

The day had gone pleasantly enough, with a short walk taking place in the afternoon. The air had been very cold and there had still been frost on the ground, but Lucius had relished the way his feet crunched over the grass. There had been plenty of conversation and much laughter, which Lucius had enjoyed a great deal. Even then, he recalled, he had always been aware of where Miss Ainsley had been in relation to him. No doubt it came from his attempts to stay far from her so she would not find him at all irritating, but all the same, he had still been very careful to note where she was... much as he was doing now.

"Let us play another game." Again, as she had done the previous two evenings, Lady Meyrick rose to her feet, and the conversations slowly began to die away. "Yes, it is another parlor game, and yes, there is some ridiculousness about it, but I am hopeful that, come tomorrow evening at the ball, we will have had enough of parlor games and be very eager to dance instead. Although," she giggled, appearing more like a young woman than the mother of a Duke, "what I *shall* tell you is there is to be a bullet pudding the night after the ball. You see, we are not finished with parlor games as yet!"

Lucius looked around the room, seeing how everyone reacted to such news. The young ladies, on the whole, laughed, with some pressing their faces to their hands at the thought of what embarrassment might be theirs. Miss Ainsley, he noted, had dropped her head, hiding her expression from everyone.

"Yes, yes, I am sure some will tell me it is not quite time for such things, but I could not wait until the twelfth night. So thus, we are to have a bullet pudding in two days' time... and we shall see who the king and the queen for a night and a day will be."

Resisting the urge to roll his eyes, Lucius kept his gaze fixed on Lady Meyrick, fighting against the urge to look across the room to Miss Ainsley again and reminding himself that Lady Borthwick was sitting on the opposite side of the room. Why was it he wanted to see her reaction rather than looking at Lady Borthwick? It seemed very strange indeed.

"For this evening, however, we shall play 'Up Jenkins'. I have two tables being set up in the library as we speak, since there are so many of us. Shall we make our way there at once?"

Everyone moved quickly and Lucius found himself hurried towards the library, finding himself rather pleased with the idea of playing 'Up Jenkins'. It was an excellent game, but also gave him the opportunity to grasp the hands of whichever young lady he was sitting beside. Usually, in fact, there would be one on either side of him, unless he was given the seat at the end of the table. There would be much laughter, and a good deal of teasing and blushes, no doubt, which to him, made for an excellent evening. A grin plastered itself across his face as he was directed towards one of the tables by Lady Meyrick. He sat down quickly, right in the middle of the row of chairs, only to turn his head and see Miss Ainsley being directed to sit beside him.

There was a stiffness to her frame that spoke of discomfort, and Lucius felt the same tension begin to run through his bones. Finding something stuck in his throat, he cleared it roughly, then turned his head away, looking directly across the table.

"How very pleasant it is to be sitting by you, Lord Northwick."

Lucius twisted his head to the other side, aware he had not even looked to see who would be sitting there with him. Lady Borthwick was all smiles, her eyes dazzling him with a clear and obvious excitement that Lucius found entirely absent from his own heart.

"Pleasant indeed, Lady Borthwick." Forcing a smile, he blinked rapidly and took in a breath as he once more set his gaze directly ahead of him, confused as to why he was feeling so many conflicting things. He ought to be delighted he was sitting next to Lady Borthwick, glad he would soon be able to grasp her hand but now, he felt as though he ought to do nothing of the sort, given that he was sitting with Miss Ainsley on the other side of him. Perhaps it was also to do with the fact that the younger Miss Ainsley sat on the opposite side of the table, although she gave no flicker of concern as to *his* presence, of course.

"I am sure we all know how to play 'Up Jenkins'." Lady Meyrick clapped her hands so as to dim the noise, her voice high and filled with enthusiasm. "One side of the tables will have a coin and must pass it between the hands of those on the opposite side. The person at the top of the table on the *other* side – that will be you, Lord Rutledge, and you also Lord Stone – must cry 'Up Jenkins'. Those who are seated with the coin on their side must then lift their hands, with them being curled into fists, and set them on the table. Those on the opposing side shall observe them carefully and must guess which person has the coin .If you guess correctly, then your side shall gain the coin, but if you fail, then it will stay with the other side! We will make certain to count the number of points each side has by the end of the evening... and those who fail shall have forfeits."

Rather than feeling any sort of delight at this, Lucius' stomach dropped to the floor. He had considered before the idea of attempting to excuse himself from any game where he might be forced to take a forfeit from Miss Bettina Ainsley, and given she now sat across the table from him, her eyes bright, perhaps he ought to consider it again - but it was not as though he could simply refuse to play, get up from his chair and excuse himself by walking from the room. The game was already set. The players were ready. To excuse himself now would ruin everything entirely.

"You need not think I would blame you for this situation, Lord Northwick." Lucius stared visibly as Miss Jane Ainsley spoke to him directly, leaning towards him so her shoulder brushed against his. "In fact, it seems I must give you the benefit of the doubt, as regards to the masquerade ball."

Lucius twisted his head sharply and Miss Ainsley dropped her gaze immediately, only to peek up at him again, her face slowly filling with color as she continued.

"If you say you did not mean to grasp at my sister the night of the ball, that you did so accidentally, then as I have said, I should believe you. It seems now I must trust that you *were*, in fact, looking for Lady Borthwick."

When she offered him a warm, delicate smile that lit up her features entirely, sending sparks of light into her green eyes, Lucius found his heart slamming against his chest. Having been entirely unused to seeing such a thing on her face, he was captivated suddenly by just how quickly it changed her appearance. He could find nothing to say, his words caught somewhere between his mouth and his mind. Had she always been this beautiful? Why had he never seen it in her before?

There was a good deal of conversation and laughter continuing around the table as Lady Meyrick realized she had no coins for the game and immediately rang for the maid to go and fetch them – for they were apparently very specific coins that must be used – leaving Lucius and Miss Ainsley with some time still to speak. And yet, he could not find anything to say.

"You appear to be rather stoic, Lord Northwick." The smile that had been on Miss Ainsley's face quickly began to disappear and the urge to see it again, to keep it in place, had Lucius' voice return to him.

"I am a little surprised, Miss Ainsley, to hear such words

from you, but I can assure you I am greatly relieved by them." Caught by her gaze, he looked into her eyes without having any intention – or even ability – to look away. "I can assure you that I never had any thought of dragging your sister away that evening. I have no plan to behave in a discourteous manner towards her here, either."

Miss Ainsley nodded, but then turned her head away. "I am relieved to hear it, although I confess I am still very aware of your reputation, Lord Northwick."

"My reputation? It is not as unfavorable as all that, surely! I am just the same as any other gentleman of the *ton*."

Seeing the lift of her brow, he quickly explained. "I have never once caused a scandal – and you may speak to my friends to confirm it, for they will tell you I have never *once* gone near a debutant, either. Yes, I admit to being a little flirtatious and stealing a lady's attentions now and again, but it is only if the lady is willing *and* if she is in a..." Fighting for the right word, his chest tightened at Miss Ainsley's frown, "in a suitable situation. I am always very cautious, Miss Ainsley."

She tilted her head at him, but there was still no smile on her lips. "Then you are a rogue with a conscience."

At this, Lucius quickly shook his head. He did not like to be given such a title and for whatever reason, he certainly did not like to hear it from the lady next to him.

"I would state I am not a rogue at all, in fact," he remarked, his jaw squaring as she shook her head. "I may have been a little wilder in my younger days, but such behavior is to be expected of *any* gentleman. To think I am somehow worse than any other gentleman is foolishness."

"But it is not as though you have any intention to wed, however," she remarked as surprise stayed Lucius' response.

"Everyone knows Lord Northwick would not be eager to court any young lady, for he would have much rather flirt and tease as many ladies as he can." With a toss of her head, her auburn curls bouncing, she looked away. "We need not be friends, Lord Northwick – in fact, I think we shall not be. But let us be amiable at least. Your reputation, regardless of your attempts to defend it, is one that will linger on regardless, and therefore, I shall never think you suitable company."

Finding what she had stated to be most disagreeable, Lucius dropped his head and shook it hard. "You do not even know me," he shot back, fighting to keep a hold of his temper that had flared so very quickly. "You have decided on my supposed reputation that I am not worthy, despite the fact I have done nothing to either you or your sister to deserve your scorn. I assure you, I am not so much a rogue as you might think me."

Miss Ainsley turned her head to look into his eyes, steel flashing. She opened her mouth to say something more – but at that very moment, the maid returned, and immediately, the games began.

Lucius composed himself with difficulty, struggling to tear the frustration from his expression and replace it with a smile. It was a very simple game, but one which required a good deal of concentration, for hands were forever fumbling under the table and one had to make certain to grasp the coin when it was given to you, for fear of dropping it to the floor! Concentration was, at present, something Lucius lacked, aware he was hot with irritation over Miss Ainsley's words to him. He wanted very much to be able to ignore her completely, to forget she was sitting next to him, but found he could not. His anger continued to bubble, furious and fierce.... until her hand touched his.

Lucius could not explain it. It was as though somebody pinned him to his seat, tying his ankles to the legs of the chair, his hands stilling in his lap. The shock of what he felt was so significant that, when the cry, 'Up Jenkins' came, it took him a little longer than the others to lift his hands. This, of course, meant they believed *he* had the coin, but since it was entirely absent from his hands, the round was won and the game began again.

"I think you should have the coin this time, Lord Northwick." Lady Borthwick leaned against him heavily, her hand reaching for his under the table. The coin was pressed into his palm, her fingers lingering over his for a little longer, her breath warming his cheek. "They will not believe it is you since they have only just guessed you the last time."

As Lucius closed the coin in his hand, Lady Borthwick smiled and looked away, but almost instantly, her thumb began to brush across his knuckles. Back and forth it went for some moment before she was forced to speak to the gentleman on her other side.

To Lucius' utter astonishment, there was not even the smallest flicker of interest in what Lady Borthwick so clearly offered him. Was this not what he had been hoping for? But the desire to pursue it was almost entirely absent! Before he could think on it longer, however, Miss Ainsley ran her fingers over his, giving the appearance of passing the coin – and everything within Lucius began to burn all at once. It was as though a whirlwind had run straight through him, twisting him this way and that, confusing everything he thought he knew about his own desires, only to show him he had no real eagerness for Lady Borthwick at all.

It was this realization that had him catching his breath, a coldness passing over him. When Lady Borthwick turned to him again and smiled, Lucius could not bring even a single flicker to his expression. It was most extraordinary and certainly not something he could understand. Why would he have no interest in Lady Borthwick? Ever since her whisper to him at the masquerade ball, he had been almost desperate for her to extend the same invitation and now, it seemed, she was beginning to do exactly what he had prayed for – so why now did he have no eagerness for her company? Why was there no quickening of his heart nor thrill of anticipation? And why had it come only when Miss Ainsley touched his hand?

"Up Jenkins!"

The call was given, and yet again, Lucius was a few moments behind everyone else in lifting his hands. This was caught by the observing side, with Miss Harding declaring that she believed this time, it *had* to be Lucius who held the coin. Perhaps the opposing side was using the previous mistake to their advantage, she suggested, and, of course, was proven correct and the coin had to be given up. Amidst many groans and cries of frustration, Lucius quickly got up from the table.

"Are you quite well, Lord Northwick?"

"I am quite well," he answered Lady Borthwick, trying to ignore the fact Miss Ainsley was looking up at him also. "I did wonder if there would be time to pour a brandy or whiskey for those who wished it." It was not his place to ask for such a thing, of course, given he was not the host, but the Duke of Meyrick clearly took no offense, for he rose immediately.

"An excellent idea!" he declared, throwing out his arms wide. "Why do we not take a short respite, Mama? We can come back to this game afterward if we so wish."

Thankfully, Lady Meyrick appeared to think this was a good idea also, and soon Lucius was not the only one who found himself standing. To his surprise, however, Lady Borthwick rose and immediately linked her arm through his before he had even a moment to speak.

And yet, no gladness filled him at her warm company.

"I am partial to a small glass of brandy, on occasion, particularly when we are almost in the depths of winter!" Her eyes twinkled as she looked up at him, giving him a somewhat coy smile. "I hope you will oblige me?"

"Of course." Turning in so that they might walk together to the opposite side of the room, his eyes caught sight of Miss Ainsley standing alone, near to the brandy table, having obviously and very quickly, retreated here. Lucius' chest tightened, for she was looking directly at him. When he caught her gaze, she dropped her head and looked away, perhaps a little embarrassed to have been seen staring.

The strange feeling, the odd sensation that had filled him when she had touched his hand, came back with such strength that Lucius was forced to catch his breath. This particular young lady had insulted him, refusing to believe he was not the rogue she thought him. Why now should he have any sort of desire to grow near to her? To be back beside her again? Unable to keep his eyes from watching her, he saw her face flush red.

She is an enigma.

Taking a breath, Lucius forced his attention elsewhere. If he could, he would think on her a little later, but for the moment all that was required of him was to accompany Lady Borthwick to fetch a brandy and thereafter, to enjoy time in her company. Mayhap, if he did so, the expectation and anticipation he had lost would return to him just as swiftly, for that was the only thing he wanted, was it not?

CHAPTER SIX

"*I* am so very excited!"

"There are to be many balls during this house party," their mother smiled as she, Bettina, and Jane made their way towards the ballroom. "I have heard the Duke of Meyrick intends to throw one every sennight! Imagine such a thing!"

With a laugh, Jane shook her head. "No, indeed, I cannot! It will be almost like we are back in the summer Season. This house party is already quite extraordinary given its size – and I am certain this will not be the only surprise the Duke has for us."

"I am sure it will not be." Lady Wilkinson reached out to grasp both of her daughter's hands. "This is a wonderful opportunity for you both to become better acquainted with some wonderful gentlemen – gentlemen you will then see again in the summer Season. Given that they will know you are connected to the Duke of Meyrick, it will be all the better for you, I am sure."

Jane shared a look with her sister, a wry smile on her lips, for she had no doubt her mother's words were particularly directed towards her, since she would have to find her match this summer, or fear becoming a spinster.

"I am sure you are right, Mama." Seeking to change the subject so she would not have to consider the matter, Jane took in a breath, aware of the flutter of butterflies in her stomach. "Let us hope our dance cards will be filled rather quickly!"

"They will be filled within a few minutes," their mother stated firmly, sending a thrill of concern through Jane. "I think you will both have many a gentleman squabbling over you. As I have stated," she finished, with a flourish. "This is an excellent opportunity."

For the first time in as many days, Jane did not immediately think of Lord Northwick as she stepped into the ballroom. With the many additional guests, it was very crowded indeed – it seemed no-one turned down an invitation from the Duke of Meyrick, not even when it was very cold and wintery outside.

"Ah, the most beautiful ladies of the evening have arrived!" Lord Ossington hurried forward quickly, as though he had anticipated their arrival. After a bow, he extended his hands, one towards Bettina and one towards Jane.

"Good evening, Lord Ossington," Jane began, but Lord Ossington interrupted her. "I beg your pardon, but might I beg your dance cards from you both? I should be very glad to be the *first* to put my name there."

Glancing at her sister, Jane slipped hers from her wrist and handed it to Lord Ossington. "Yes, of course."

"But not you, Miss Ainsley!"

Much to Jane's surprise, none other than Lord Northwick came to stand by Lord Ossington, reaching to take Bettina's dance card from her fingers before Lord Ossington could do so. Jane swallowed hard, hearing the laughter and seeing the smiles around her, but finding nothing within herself except a slowly growing sense of dread. What was it Lord Northwick would ask of Bettina?

"Your silver hairpin, Miss Ainsley!" Lord Northwick chuckled, handing her back her trinket. "And in return, I must ask to choose whatever dance I wish from your dance card."

Bettina laughed, Lord Ossington held up both hands as though to permit it, and the dread in Jane's stomach faded away into something more, something that sank into her heart and made her frown.

Unless I am a little jealous?

Disliking such a thought, Jane hastily threw it away. Of course, she was not jealous. She did not like Lord Northwick, did not find him appealing in any way. Why would she care if he danced with her sister and not with her?

He has done as he stated, I suppose.

Jane took in a deep breath and forced a smile as Lord Ossington handed back her dance card. He had taken the quadrille, which would be upon them very soon.

"The quadrille, Miss Ainsley."

Jane looked across as Lord Northwick handed the dance card back to Bettina. He had taken the very same dance Lord Ossington had taken for her, meaning all of her other dances were free. It was then that Lord Northwick extended his hands towards Jane herself, his eyebrow lifting slightly as if he was challenging her.

"I should not like to appear rude by dancing with only one sister. If I may?"

With fumbling fingers, Jane held out her dance card, jerking as his fingers touched hers. It was brief, but still long enough for her to react. She did not know what it was about him that made her respond so, but a strange sense of burning heat began to pour from the top of her head down to her toes as Lord Northwick held her gaze. Somehow, she feared he knew exactly what she was thinking, and yet she still could not look away. Eventually, it was Lord Northwick who broke their gaze, looking down at her dance cards so he might write his name somewhere. Jane's stomach began to churn as he hovered his pencil over the card. Whatever was taking him so long? Mayhap, she considered, he was looking for whichever dance would be the shortest, so they would not have to spend long in each other's company. As far as she was concerned, he was only going to dance with her, so he would not appear rude. As her nerves began to swirl all the more, Jane took in a deep breath, silently praying her torment might soon be over.

"There, Miss Ainsley." With a quick smile, Lord Northwick handed the dance card back to her with a small inclination of his head. Jane slipped it quickly onto her wrist without even looking to see which one it was he had taken, suddenly both nervous and anxious over what was, of course, such a small thing. The two gentlemen smiled and, as yet more approached, were quickly forced to take their leave. Jane continued to look straight ahead, not looking down at her dance card again till finally, she could take it no longer. Relieved that Lord Northwick had by now turned away, she swiped it from her wrist and turned it over, seeing his name there.

Astonishment bloomed through her, sending the nerves in her stomach wriggling through her veins. Why had he chosen to take her waltz? The waltz was certainly not the shortest of dances and would gain a good deal more attention than some of the other ones. He had obviously been deliberate in his choice, and yet she simply could not understand it.

Did he not want their dance to be over as soon as it could? Why, then, would he pick something so obvious? Was it because he knew she would be highly embarrassed by their closeness during the waltz?

She had no time to linger on such feelings or thoughts, however, for other gentlemen were soon at her side, asking for her dance card, although Jane found herself giving none of them more than the briefest consideration. The only person she thought of was Lord Northwick, finding herself gazing absently across the room, as though somehow she might be able to silently communicate her surprise and curiosity to him if their gazes were to meet. If he thought to embarrass her, then she would prove to him she had no such feelings when it came to dancing the waltz, even if it was with a gentleman she did not much like.

Or perhaps the gentleman makes me feel things that I cannot easily push away.

Her frame shook with such a thought and, to distract herself, Jane found herself looking down at what would be a very busy evening, for now, all of her dances were taken. Her gaze went to the waltz once more, seeing Lord Northwick's name there. Straightening, she lifted her chin. Once the waltz was at an end, then she would be able to enjoy the rest of the evening without hesitation. It was only a dance. She need not concern herself with anything else. She would dance with Lord Northwick, would set it aside, and then continue on with the other gentlemen. There was nothing more to think of.

. . .

Before she knew it, the waltz was upon her, and to Jane's frustration, she was nothing but nervous. This was not how she wanted to appear. She wanted to seem calm and collected, as though this dance was nothing of any consequence when inwardly, she was a puddle of anxiety.

Lord Northwick appeared suddenly next to her, surprising Jane so much, she started violently.

"Forgive me, Lord Northwick." Keeping her smile pinned to her features. "I was just a little surprised at how quickly the waltz had come about. This evening has gone rather quickly, has it not?"

Lord Northwick merely smiled. "I suppose it has." He said nothing more until they stepped together to the dance floor, surrounded by the other couples who had also come to dance the waltz. The music began, as though it had been waiting for the two of them to step out together. A little perturbed over how dry her mouth now was, Jane stepped forward into his arms.

The nearness of him was overpowering.

A scent of pine surrounded her as she began the steps. It was a rather pleasant scent, reminding her of the trees on her father's grounds on a crisp spring morning. Despite her nervousness, she allowed a genuine smile to brush her lips.

"I saw your smile," Lord Northwick murmured. "It is not as bad as you have feared, I think, dancing with me."

Jane, who had been looking over his shoulder, threw him a glance. It was barely a look, but what she saw in his eyes made her heart lift and quail, all at the same time. There was a smile on his face, which she had not seen before, and a light in his expression, which seemed to speak of joy. Why she was responding in such a way to his nearness, she could not find an explanation for. She ought to be counting every moment, wishing it would pass with an even greater swiftness, and instead she was now eager for the waltz to go on, so she could spend a little longer in his arms.

It was all very strange indeed.

A sudden thought made her face burn. Yes, Lord Northwick had said he would not go near a debutant, but then again, she was not a debutant, was she? She would be in her third season and certainly was not in the first flush of youth. She could not be one of his conquests, could she?

To her utter horror, her heart seemed to desire such a thing. It was as though a great part of her wished to be close to him, as if somehow, he was becoming dear to her.

No, that was foolishness. She ought to be thinking *only* of gentlemen who had a promising future ahead of them, someone who was eager to marry. Such a thing could never be said about Lord Northwick, for everyone in London was aware he was nothing more than a flirt, with no firm plans to attach himself to anyone.

"Your face is a little flushed." Lord Northwick leaned a little closer, sending Jane's heart into palpitations. "Are you quite all right?"

"I am well." Closing her eyes for a moment, she forced her concentration to focus solely on the music. Her fingers seemed to curl around his a little tighter, solely of their own accord, as the dance began to come to an end. It was as if they were eager to cling to him, even though she herself was barely able to look into his face.

Eventually, he stepped back and Jane was forced to release his hand, her body cooling as they moved apart. "It seems as though we are going from friends to enemies and back again," Lord Northwick remarked as he offered her his arm to walk her back to the side of the ballroom. "We are never balanced, I think. I had hoped this waltz would offer a chance to talk, but obviously..."

Jane nodded. "I do not want any animosity between us, Lord Northwick," she found herself saying. "Truly, I do not."

"Then we shall be amiable." He threw her a smile. "Shall we promise not to fight any longer? State we shall not share another cross word, even if we are nothing more than... acquaintances."

Jane swallowed hard. "I thank you." Her heart catapulted across her chest as he reached across to press her hand as it rested on his arm.

"You have nothing to thank me for, Miss Ainsley. That will do very well indeed."

CHAPTER SEVEN

"This is a most excellent Christmas ball, is it not?"

Lucius smiled as Lord Renforth grinned at him.

"Yes, indeed it is," he agreed, without any hesitation. "The Duke has outdone himself."

"And I hear there is to be another one in a sennight," Lord Renforth exclaimed, making Lucius' brows lift in surprise.

"You mean to say there will be another ball in only a few days' time?" Seeing his friend nodding eagerly, Lucius found himself chuckling. "Good gracious, the Duke of Meyrick is very eager to enjoy this time of year, is he not?"

"And who could blame him?" Lord Renforth gestured towards the window, which showed nothing but the darkness outside. "It is cold. It becomes dark very early and we find ourselves in the midst of a freezing winter – and yet there is a great deal of joy and delight to be found here, lifting our spirits and freeing us from the gloom. I, for one, am very eager indeed to step out again at another ball."

"But no doubt you will be spending most of the time dancing with your wife," Lucius remarked, seeing his friend grin. "I, however, must make certain I dance with every young lady present during the course of the house party, so I do not show any one of them particular favor and, at the same time, make certain not to insult any of them by my absence!"

Lord Renforth chuckled. "A difficulty, indeed," he stated dryly. "Although I did see that you did not dance any of them underneath the mistletoe bough." Motioning with his chin, he drew Lucius' attention to where the mistletoe bough was held, but Lucius only shook his head. There had been a temptation to do so, of course, but he had found himself only interested in stealing a kiss from *one* of the ladies he had danced with. He had been very able to lead Miss Ainsley towards the mistletoe bough had he chosen to but for some reason, the strength of feeling he had over the idea had been so fierce that he had turned away from it entirely, fearful of what would take place if he permitted himself to do so.

"Well, if you shall not, then I am certain many others will."

Hearing something in Lord Renforth's voice, Lucius looked back again towards the mistletoe bough, only to see Lord Ossington press a kiss to Miss Jane Ainsley's cheek. Upon seeing this, Lucius was filled with such a fierce fire that he was forced to drag in air to quench it, discomfited at how his hands curled into fists, his frame stiffening.

"Are you quite well?" Concern flooded his friend's voice as Lucius nodded, dragging his eyes away.

"Yes, of course."

Lord Renforth's frown lingered for some moments

more, but seeing Lucius was not about to give any explanation, he shrugged and looked away. "We were talking of how magnificent all of this is," he reminded Lucius, seeming to understand the need to pull Lucius back to the conversation. "And the arrival of Lady Borthwick has excited many a fellow, I must say." This last remark was followed with the lift of his eyebrow, but Lucius ignored it, shrugging both shoulders as though he had no intention of even *noticing* what his friend was saying about Lady Borthwick. The truth was, of course, he still had a great many conflicting feelings over the lady and, as yet, was unable to decipher one from the other.

"Rumor has it she has set her eyes upon one or two gentlemen here at this house party," Lord Renforth continued, still keeping a steady gaze fixed on Lucius who forced himself to hold it, not willing to allow even the smallest flicker to his expression. "Has she given you any hint of interest? I know her nearness is what you were hopeful for during the summer season, as you yourself have told me!"

Lucius opened his mouth, then closed it again, snapping back his response. He was not yet entirely sure where his mysterious note had come from, even though his belief was that it had been from Lady Borthwick. He had had no assurance as yet and therefore, did not want to say anything openly to Lord Renforth.

"I could not say specifically. I –"

Sticking his hand in his pocket, Lucius' words ran dry as he felt something there, something he had no knowledge of placing in his pocket. Taking it out, he saw it was yet another note, although this time, there was no ribbon tied around it.

"What is it you have there?" Clearly rather intrigued,

Lord Renforth leaned forward as Lucius unfolded the note, only to stare down at it, his heart slamming against his ribs as shock rippled over him.

"I cannot believe this." With his voice low, Lucius read the note over and over again, hardly able to take in what it said. There was a promise of embraces, of kisses, of softness and warmth... and yet it was signed by Miss Ainsley. The last line begged him to meet her in the library an hour after the ball had ended.

"This cannot be." Shaking his head, Lucius folded up the note and pushed it back into his pocket again. "There must be some explanation for this."

"If I were you, I should burn the note." Lord Renforth tapped his arm, suddenly looking very grave indeed. "You should not want it to fall into the wrong hands."

Lucius shoved his fingers through his hair, blowing out a long breath as he did so. "It cannot be from Miss Ainsley," he muttered, glancing at his friend. "Miss Ainsley has made it quite clear there is nothing of interest between us – the elder, I mean. Miss Jane Ainsley does not much like my company, as you are very well aware." Yes, they had resolved things a little, and they were to be amiable at least, but that did not mean she would have *ever* written him something such as this! "And the younger Miss Ainsley has barely spoken to me – nor I to her."

"Could it be some sort of test, then?" Lord Renforth suggested, a small frown across his brow. "I know you have been determined to prove to Miss Ainsley you have no interest in her sister and are a gentleman who can be respected in that regard -,"

"*And* that I made a mistake at the masquerade ball," Lucius interrupted. "Then it could be an attempt to prove she knows *precisely* what sort of fellow I am, even though I claim to be something else." The more he considered this, the more sense it seemed to make. "It is a possibility, certainly. If it is from the lady, then I certainly will not be taken in by it!" His chest puffed out, indignation rising. "In fact, I will speak to her directly."

His friend grabbed his arm. "Are you quite certain such a thing is wise? Why do not both you *and* I make our way to the library? If it is Miss Ainsley who has written the note, then she will see us both and you will be able to confront her then. And if it is not she who is standing there waiting for you, then you may find yourself in a much more pleasant situation."

Lucius shook his head. There was something about this that made his anger burn, quite certain what Lord Renforth had suggested was the only explanation for the note, for who else would have done such a thing? If it was a ploy, then he would speak to the lady about it at once. Shaking off Lord Renforth's grasping hand, he made his way carefully through the crowd and attempted to find the lady in question.

It did not take long for him to spot her.

"Miss Ainsley." He did not so much as incline his head, but came to stand directly in front of her, interrupting her conversation without hesitation. Miss Ainsley's eyes flared in shock and it took some moments for her to reply, but when she did, it was with a slight tilt of her chin, showing no concern over his sudden presence.

"Lord Northwick." Her voice was calm. "You have come to speak to me with great eagerness, it seems. Are you quite well?"

Ignoring the others around her, Lucius jerked his head

to the left. "Might I have a word in private, Miss Ainsley?" he asked, his tone giving her no opportunity to argue. "Let us step away just over here, so you remain in sight of your sister."

She blinked but, after a moment, assented, excusing herself gracefully.

"Whatever is the matter? Why do you interrupt me so?" Genuine concern seemed to fill her voice as she joined him, standing only a few steps away from those she had been talking with. "Is there something wrong? What has happened?"

Lucius drew in a deep breath, filling his chest with air as he looked into her face. Her green eyes were wide, her alabaster skin appearing a little paler than usual, but he merely shook his head, refusing to believe the sight of innocence laid before him.

"I will ask you this only once, Miss Ainsley." With great deliberation, he pulled the note from his pocket and waved it at her. "Why would you put *this* in my pocket?"

Miss Ainsley did not make a single sound, her gaze travelling first to the note and then back to his face, but there was no immediate, sharp response, nor a defense of ignorance.

Lucius put both hands to his waist, his elbows akimbo, with the note tucked between his fingers. "Miss Ainsley?"

Miss Ainsley took in a deep breath. "I am afraid I have no understanding of what this is," she said quietly, her tone soft where his was hard. "You appear to believe I know something of whatever it is you are flapping at me, but I can assure you I have none."

Closing his eyes briefly, Lucius blew out a long breath. "You think I will believe you know nothing about the note?"

Miss Ainsley frowned. "I thought we had agreed to be amiable towards each other, Lord Northwick. Why now are you coming at me with such anger?" Her question hung in the air between them, and Lucius drew in another breath, trying to keep his temper in check. Was she either playing the part of innocence, or was there any truth to her words?

"I believe you placed this in my pocket in the hope I would prove myself to be the rogue you think me." Yet again, he waved the note around in his hand but was unprepared for the sharp response of Miss Ainsley, who reached out and grasped it with one hand. Before he could snatch it back, she had unfolded it, reading the few lines... and Lucius heard her snatch of breath.

When she looked up at him, Lucius' determination faltered. The concern shining in her eyes, the gasp of surprise, and the way she stepped closer to him spoke of complete and utter astonishment.

It was not her.

"Where did you get this?"

Lucius shook his head, mute with shame. Miss Ainsley moved all the closer, one hand going to his arm, her grip rather tight around his wrist. "I must understand, Lord Northwick, wherever did you get such a note? I can assure you I did not pen it." Taking a deep breath, she squeezed his wrist a little harder. "And it is certainly not from my sister."

Licking his lips, Lucius wished that he might go back a few minutes and tell himself to take some time before he spoke. He had reacted sharply and now, it seemed, he had been entirely mistaken. A heavy sigh broke from him and he dropped his head.

"Forgive me, Miss Ainsley. I thought you had placed it there yourself," he explained, choosing to be entirely honest. "I thought it would be a test for me, a test to prove I had no intention of seeking out your sister. But it is now clear you nor your sister have written it. I find myself quite at a loss."

Miss Ainsley looked back at him, her eyes still wide, the edge of her lip caught between her teeth. Her eyes closed, air rasping out between her lips. "As do I."

Nothing passed between them for some moments other than a look. Aware of the warmth of embarrassment settling in his chest, Lucius was the first to pull his gaze away. He ought to have been more considerate, but instead had laid this at her feet, suspecting her to be worthy of such cruelty. Was that not what she had done to him? She had blamed him for pulling her sister away, had stated he had done so deliberately, even though he had protested his innocence – and now here he stood, stating precisely the same thing to her.

At least she had cause for such belief.

A wry smile pulled at his lips and he shook his head. "Miss Ainsley, I must apologize." When her eyes lifted to his with obvious and evident surprise, he simply spread out both hands. "I should not have thought so of you, nor come to speak with you in such a demanding manner. I have no reason to believe you would be so vicious, especially when you yourself have only just spoken of your desire for us to be amiable to each other."

Something flashed in her eyes, but she did not smile. "I thank you for your apology, Lord Northwick. No doubt you believed that in doing such a thing, it would prove to both myself and to you that what I thought of your character was correct. But I assure you, I would never be so scheming."

It was as if she spoke to his very heart, and his embarrassment grew to shame. He did not deserve her hasty forgiveness.

"This does concern me, however," she continued, as though the last few minutes had not taken place. "Why would someone sign my name – or my sister's name – to a note such as this?"

"It will be nothing more than some sort of foolish game – a game known only to whoever has written the letter." Taking a breath, he shrugged. "Mayhap this lady delights in being hidden, perhaps thinking she appears coquettish in doing so. Therefore, she has put whoever's name came to mind and, unfortunately, it was yours.

Miss Ainsley's lips twisted. "It may not be a lady," she suggested, speaking a little more slowly as thoughts came to her. "Mayhap it is one of your friends, thinking to tease you and eager to take advantage of your willingness to believe such things. Perhaps when you go to library this evening, you will not find a lady of quality waiting for you, but a gentleman who will then laugh at your surprise and frustration when there *is* no lady waiting for you." Her shoulders lifted. "A prank, perhaps."

Lucius considered this for some moments, saying nothing but silently beginning to see the wisdom in such a suggestion. This house party had been filled with teasing and games thus far, so why should this not be a continuation of such things?

"I would not put such a thing past the likes of Lord Rosenthal, or even Lord Kingsley." Admitting this aloud, Miss Ainsley gave him a small smile, although it did not light her eyes. Rather, she seemed a little pained as she looked away from him.

"Whomever it is. Lord Northwick, might you ask them not to use my sister's name nor my own name again? It could have caused a great deal of scandal had someone else seen it."

Surprising himself by his action. Lucius reached out and pressed her hand gently. It was but a moment, but within that moment, molten heat seemed to burst from his core, pushing itself through every part of his being. He could give no explanation for it. Swallowing hard, he looked back at Miss Ainsley, wondering if she felt anything similar, but her expression remained the same.

Evidently, she did not feel the same heat as he.

"I understand your concern," he told her, quickly taking his hand away. "Of course, I will not say a word."

Miss Ainsley pressed her hand to her heart. "I very much appreciate your concern., Lord Northwick."

Buoying himself also more, he lifted his chest high. "In fact, I shall burn this note immediately." So saying, he walked across the ballroom towards the fireplace, which was located at the far end. Miss Ainsley came to join him and, without a second thought, Lucius tossed the note in. Together, they watched as it burned up into dust and ashes, the heat billowing towards them... but it was not the heat from the fire that burned in his veins.

He glanced towards Miss Ainsley, catching the way her cheeks flushed, although her expression still bore a small frown. The desire to reassure her become insurmountable, and he leaned towards her, waiting until her eyes turned to his before he spoke.

"It is done." Glancing over his shoulder, he tilted his head. "The only other person who knows of this is Lord Renforth, and I can assure you he will be discretion itself."

At this, Miss Ainsley smiled quickly, although it was only fleeting. "I thank you."

To Lucius' eye, it appeared she was still troubled and thus, he spoke the words of concern that were building in his heart. "Something still worries you, I think."

Her eyes flashed away, then returned to him. "Yes, I confess I am." Sighing, she turned, a little aware of the fire. "You have given me your explanation as to who would have written the note using my name, but I admit, I continue to wonder who would have done so – and what their purpose might be."

Lucius smiled gently. "You have no enemies, I think?"

She shook her head.

"Then trust me when I say this will be nothing more than either foolishness on the part of one of my friends, or the work of someone eager to hide their identity from me for the present, perhaps thinking it will somehow make them a little more mysterious."

Miss Ainsley nodded slowly, pressing her lips together. After some moments, she pushed her shoulders back a little and nodded. "You are quite correct, Lord Northwick, of course," Her frame shook slightly as she let out another breath, and it was only then Lucius realized just how disturbed she was over the affair.

"Might you...?"

Her sentence came to a quick stop as she bit her lip and looked away from him, clearly halfway between asking something and thinking it best not to.

She still needs further reassurance.

"If you would like me to inform you as to who it is that appears this evening, I would be glad to do so, if it would put your mind at rest?"

Miss Ainsley only nodded, her gaze still twisting away.

"I did not mean to upset you," he continued, as tiny little needles of guilt bore their way into his heart. "It was not my intention."

It was this statement that had her looking straight at him and, after a second, her lips quirked in a most unexpected manner. "Even though your manner of speaking about this to me was a little unguarded and fierce, I confess I am glad to know of it." A quiet laugh reached his ears, and Lucius found himself smiling with relief at the sound of it. "In fact, I would say I am grateful! Grateful to you for telling me about this. Allow me to reiterate my desire for us both to be amiable in our connection, Lord Northwick. Your willingness to speak with me about the note has shown me your character is perhaps not as I have always considered it."

Lucius swallowed hard, finding himself both astonished and thrilled at her explanation. Having the desire to make himself appear even more gentlemanly, he inclined his head, then offered her his arm.

"Thank you, Miss Ainsley. I am appreciative of your honesty and in your consideration of me. I will not pretend I have always been gentlemanly in my behavior, but in this regard, I assure you I shall be."

Miss Ainsley smiled and took his arm before Lucius began to lead them both back in the direction of her sister. He walked slowly, enjoying the quiet moments where he might simply be in Miss Ainsley's company, while still confused over the reactions her nearness built in him.

"Good evening, Miss Ainsley. I will speak to you as soon as I can, come the morrow."

Her smile was gentle as she took her hand from his arm. "I thank you, Lord Northwick. Good evening."

Depositing her by her sister, Lucius immediately went in search of Lord Renforth. There were several things he had to make clear to his friend, with the first and most important being that Miss Ainsley had *not* been the one to put the note in his pocket. Thereafter, he wished to ask Lord Renforth to accompany him to the library in the hour after the ball, in the hope that whoever had written the note would reveal themselves, just as they had said.

But he would not be taken in, would not even open his arms to any lady who came to the library this evening. The idea held no pleasure, for when he thought of holding a lady close, the only person he wanted was Miss Jane Ainsley.

CHAPTER EIGHT

"I must speak with you, Bettina."

Her sister came to a sudden stop as she walked into the bedchamber, seeming to expect Jane to berate her about something, but Jane quickly waved a hand. "It is nothing you have done, my dear sister. It is only to warn you that something malevolent may be happening here. It is to do with Lord Northwick."

"Lord Northwick?" Her sister's eyes went wide as she went to sit down on the edge of her bed. "Surely you cannot be thinking of him again. My dear sister, you must forget him and all you think of him. I am sure everything he has said about the masquerade ball is quite true."

Jane laughed and quickly shook her head. "You will be surprised to hear this, I am sure, but Lord Northwick and I actually had a pleasant conversation."

Bettina's eyes grew even wider.

"Yes, you may be astonished but it is quite true."

"I knew you danced," Bettina replied slowly. "Did you speak then?"

Jane blinked as bumps broke out all over her skin, as

though she were recalling what it was like to have been in his arms. "No, we did not have much opportunity to speak." Turning away so her sister would not see the flush that Jane was sure had broken out over her cheeks, she continued quickly. "He came to ask me about a note. Lord Northwick was concerned about it."

Her sister rubbed her hands over her bare arms, and Jane glanced at the fire. It was already beginning to die down which meant they should change and be in their beds before it died completely. "Allow me to quickly explain," she continued hastily. "Someone had placed a note in Lord Northwick's pocket and the note was signed 'Miss Ainsley'."

Taking a breath, she waited for her sister to take this in, to try and understand the severity of it.

Bettina only frowned. "I am sure such a thing was meant as a jest." She rose, ready to change out of her gown. "As our own mother has said, a Christmas House party is filled with all manner of fun. I am sure this is only one of those things."

"Bettina, there is still caution to be had here." Jane held her sister's gaze steadily, attempting to put as much meaning into her words as she could. "The note contained an invitation to Lord Northwick, asking him to a.... a meeting."

"What sort of meeting?" Bettina asked as Jane let out a groan. She was not managing to explain herself very well at all.

"The note that was pressed into Lord Northwick's pocket contained a good deal of encouragements – encouragements I would find most distressing should they ever be laid at my feet." Catching the frown that burrowed its way across her sister's forehead, Jane let out another sigh. She was going to have to speak plainly. "The person who wrote the note was seeking a dalliance, Bettina. That is why I do not believe it to have been written in jest."

At this, her sister sucked in air as Jane closed her eyes briefly, glad now her sister understood. "You see now why I am concerned. If the note had been discovered by someone else, we would have been left with a great scandal."

"Certainly now, I do!" Bettina exclaimed. "Do you mean to say Lord Northwick thought you or I would be meeting him for this..." Closing her eyes, she shook her head. "This *dalliance*." The word was spoken with disgust, as though it was the most abominable of things, and Jane let out a slow breath of relief that her sister felt the same worry as she.

"Lord Northwick believed something along those lines, although he soon learned that neither you nor I wrote such a thing. He has come to the conclusion the note is either a ploy to tease him or some sort of foolishness on the part of his friends." Choosing not to give her sister the entirety of the truth about how Lord Northwick had spoken to her at the first, for it was already growing a little colder in the room, Jane rose to her feet. "We must be very cautious indeed. Lord Northwick knows now that neither you nor I placed the note in his pocket, and I hope I shall learn *who* set it there one way or the other. But it would be best to make certain we remain always proper, regardless of the situation or the circumstances. And perhaps it would be wise if we stayed a little further away from Lord Northwick."

Bettina laughed and shook her head. "I do not think you need fear we will be in any way damaged by something such as this, Jane. If Lord Northwick is aware neither of us wrote the note, then what have we to be concerned about? I was afraid you would say there had already been a scandal caused and we would have consequences to face! But now you have told me everything. I can see there is no immediate concern."

Jane smiled softly, seeing her sister's youthful exuberance in relation to her own, more stoic outlook. "I want us both to be careful, that is all," she explained as Bettina smiled back at her. "I am doing what I can to protect you."

"Which I greatly appreciate," Bettina answered. "But I do not think we need to be too cautious. It will have been a name someone plucked from amongst many of the guests. It could have been done, as you have said yourself, to tease Lord Northwick. Perhaps they hope he will turn up to the library and find it entirely empty and will be ashamed of his hope and eagerness, or mayhap they will appear there themselves and laugh at his surprise when it is neither you nor I standing there."

Jane caught the edge of her lip between her teeth. "All the same, it has unsettled me," she said honestly. "Even though I saw Lord Northwick fling the note into the flames, I have allowed that concern to linger."

Bettina took her hand and squeezed her fingers. "You are the most wonderful sister I could ever have asked for." Embracing Jane for a long moment, Bettina let out a breath. "But you need not worry so much about me. With all the frivolity taking place at the present time, I do not think we need to have any concerns. Do try and be a little more at ease if you can."

Jane took in another breath as her sister stepped back. There was wisdom in Bettina's words, and Jane found herself nodding as her sister hurriedly began to prepare for bed. "Yes, I think you are right. I shall try." Aware of the room becoming colder by the second, Jane hastily began to prepare for bed. The sooner she could climb into bed, the sooner she could fall asleep and that, perhaps, would give her mind the rest it so desperately needed.

"WELL?"

Lord Northwick turned sharply as Jane approached, his eyes flaring as though he had not expected her to come so close.

"Good afternoon, Miss Ainsley." With a slight inclination of his head, Lord Northwick moved so he might face her. "Are you quite well?"

Jane rolled her eyes. "Pray, do not feel the need to engage yourself in polite conversation. Surely you must know why I am coming to speak with you?"

Lord Northwick frowned, only for it to clear a second later as his breath hitched. "Yes, of course. It was about the note last evening, was it not?"

"Indeed." Waiting for a few moments, Jane resisted the urge to let out a frustrated sigh, seeing a line draw itself between Lord Northwick's brows.

Whatever had happened?

"You wish to know about last evening and who it was that met me in the library." For whatever reason, Lord Northwick did not appear able to look in her direction for, as he spoke, his eyes averted.

"I should be glad to know if it would not be improper to tell me." A sudden warmth began to flood through her, burning through her skin as a flare of embarrassment lit her cheeks. What if Lord Northwick had enjoyed a dalliance with someone last evening, someone who had purported to be 'Miss Ainsley' for some reason? And now, here she was, asking him about such a thing! Little wonder he did not want to speak to her of it. Shifting slightly, she made to turn around. "My apologies. If it is a private matter, then I have no need to –"

His hand caught her wrist. "Pray do not go."

The fire in her veins grew all the hotter as she swung back to face him, wondering at her reaction to him. What was it about him that made her skin burn so? Why was it she did not find such a heat within herself when any other gentleman drew near? It was most confusing.

"It is not because I do not wish to tell you, but more because it is both confusing and embarrassing." Releasing her wrist, Lord Northwick clasped his hands behind his back, his shoulders rounding. "I went to the library, as instructed, and brought Lord Renforth with me. However, there was no one there."

Jane blinked quickly, the heated throbbing in her veins beginning to fade away. "What do you mean?"

Again, Lord Northwick looked away. "I mean precisely that: there was no one else present. I waited for some time after the designated hour, having arrived early, and no-one stepped into the library. I assume now it must have been some great prank, some teasing." A heavy sigh tore from him. "No doubt you will soon hear about amongst the ladies."

"Why ever should *I* hear about it?"

Finally, Lord Northwick's gaze rested on hers. "Because some lady amongst the group will laugh about what they have done. They will think it very mirthful indeed that I stood in the library alone, waiting for someone who did not appear. Perhaps it is. I shall have to ask you to inform me of whatever it is you hear, rather than the other way around."

Still rather confused, Jane frowned, her lips twisting as

she narrowed her gaze a little. "Do you truly believe someone would have done such a thing simply to make a mockery of you?"

"Yes, I fully believe so." Again, his shoulders lifted, but this time, they remained a little higher. There was a clear tension in what he was telling her, in what he had endured, and Jane caught herself sympathizing with him. It must have been frustrating to stand in the library without anyone arriving, and then all the more embarrassing to realize that someone, somewhere within the house party, would already be laughing at him.

"As you may be able to tell, I am a little humiliated, but perhaps the embarrassment was the point of it all."

Jane tilted her head. "Mayhap," she agreed quietly. "Although there is another possibility."

His eyebrows lifted questioningly.

"The person in question saw Lord Renforth with you and, in seeing him, decided they would not come to speak with you after all. It is an idea, is it not?"

A slow smile began to spread across Lord Northwick's face. Jane could not understand the reason for it, but when his eyes began to twinkle, she felt a blush begin to warm her cheeks.

"You have a very inquisitive and intelligent mind, Miss Ainsley. You will not accept my explanation to be the only one there could be. Already you are thinking of further possibilities."

"In the spirit of humility, I will admit to it, at least," she found herself saying. "I have been concerned, obviously, for the reputation of myself and my sister, but your assurance that I need not to be so worried has been a great support. I spoke to Bettina of it last night."

Lord Northwick nodded slowly, his smile beginning to shatter. "She must have been as surprised as you."

"Yes, she was, although she did not take it as seriously as I," Jane admitted, with a quick smile that faded in the moments after. "Instead, Bettina encouraged me to forget about the note entirely, putting it down – as you did – to the teasing and laughter that often takes place during house parties such as these."

"I am glad to hear that at least," Lord Northwick answered quietly, his hand catching hers for a very brief moment. "I do think it would be wise to put this to the side, Miss Ainsley. "And should anything happen again that might have your name attached to it, I will be very careful indeed to bring it to your attention."

At this, Jane's breath caught in her chest and she moved closer to him, her voice dropping to a whisper. "Do you mean to say this is not the first note you have received?"

The gentleman licked his lips, cleared his throat, and looked away. "No, it has not." Glancing back at her, he lifted his shoulders as though to dismiss what had happened. "The first note I received was placed on my dressing table."

Jane's eyebrows lifted higher. "Someone stepped into your bedchamber and placed it there? A lady in this very house?"

"Yes, I believe so." His gaze dropped to the floor. "The first one was not specific with a day or a time of meeting, but rather a proposal our acquaintance become a little.... closer. I was to look out for a furthering of their warm affections towards me, although I did not know what such a thing would mean." A slightly rueful laugh escaped. "Mayhap the note last evening was meant to be the fulfillment of the first, only for Lord Renforth's presence to bring it to an end before it had even begun!"

"And yet you still believed *I* was the one responsible for the note last evening?" Jane protested as Lord Northwick winced. "Good gracious, you must have thought very poorly of me indeed!" Guilt writhed immediately through her conscience, causing her to squeeze her eyes closed. "Although now I speak such things aloud, I do not think I can make any complaint in that regard, given I have done the very same to you."

"Yes, but not without cause," came the reply, the warmth on his face unmistakable. There was a softness around his eyes and a gentle smile on his lips and for the first time, Jane admitted she might well have judged Lord Northwick unfairly. Perhaps his reputation for being something of a rogue was only that – a reputation. It did not mean it had any real truth in it.

"No, I suppose, not." Murmuring quietly, she looked to one side of the room, suddenly uncomfortable and unsure of herself. She and Lord Northwick had endured nothing but difficulty in their connection the last few months, but now it was beginning to alter. She had never expected to see him at the Christmas house party and certainly had never once believed they would improve their acquaintance. It felt as though they might now be on their way to becoming friends, and quite how Jane felt about their new connection, she did not know.

"I.... I think I should like to find out a little more about what is taking place at this house party." Before she could prevent herself, she found herself saying more than she had ever expected.

"But why?" he asked her, tipping his head. "You have no concern as regards myself, surely?"

Jane blinked, uncertain as to what it was she could say by way of explanation. Was it that she felt something for Lord Northwick? Something pushing her to discover the truth alongside him?

"Now, I have told you all we are to have a bullet pudding!" Before the conversation could take any further turns – and much to Jane's relief, Lady Meyrick clapped her hands, as she always did, to gain the attention of the room. The mention of the word 'bullet pudding' made Jane's stomach churn furiously in spite of her relief, and despite the cheers and the laughter, had not even the smallest sense of anticipation.

"I do recall Lady Meyrick threatened us with such a thing some two days ago."

Jane jumped violently at just how close Lord Northwick's voice was to her ear; her skin immediately prickling with goosebumps. Swallowing against a sudden tightness in her throat, she glanced across at him.

"I confess I am not at all enthusiastic." A little confused as to why she was speaking so openly with the gentleman, she found her lips moving of their own accord. "The thought of my face covered with flour is not a pleasant one." Despite the fact she knew all too well she ought to find some merriment within herself, the consequences of losing the game would, she considered, be nothing short of mortifying.

"Well, perhaps you shall win," Lord Northwick replied, making Jane laugh a little wryly. "I do wonder what the reward shall be. With Lady Meyrick, there is always a reward!"

As though she had heard him. Lady Meyrick immediately began to answer such a question. "We shall have two bullet puddings, one for the gentleman and one for the ladies. Everyone should take turns cutting a slice of the flour. If the cake should fall and the bullet should topple, then the person shall be declared the loser, and I believe we all know the consequences of that!"

The entire room began to murmur as Jane wrapped both arms around her waist, in an attempt to stop the swirling there.

"But we shall also have a reward." Another murmur ran around the room, but Jane frowned, a little uncertain as to what Lady Meyrick meant.

"Whoever cut the cake *before* the bullet falls will be declared the winner, and then we shall have our King and our Queen of the house party!" She giggled as though she were already anticipating what was to come. "Our King and our Queen shall then be treated with great distinction, given whatever they desire, and of course shall have to rule over us for the rest of today and all of tomorrow. We shall have to do as they bid us, no matter how foolish a command it may be!"

Closing her eyes, Jane let out a slow breath she hoped no one would hear, aware of the inward groaning filling her at the thought of engaging in such nonsense. Yes, it was more foolish games, and yes, she ought to try and engage herself in it the same way as everyone else, but the thought of embarrassing herself was too great to allow her even a flicker of interest, urging her instead to escape before the frivolity began.

Except there was nowhere for her to extricate herself.

"Well, I am sure one is more preferable to the other," Lord Northfield chuckled, lightly nudging her shoulder with his in a possible attempt to make her smile, but still Jane struggled to find even the smallest sense of enthusiasm. She did not wish to have her face pushed into the flour, nor did she wish to become queen - whatever it was such a title meant – but there was to be no opportunity to even think of a reason to remove herself from the room. The door opened and the bullet puddings were carefully brought in by the household staff. Jane pitied the maids as they set their bullet puddings on the table. Should any of them make the smallest mistake, then the bullet pudding would be ruined – and they would get the blame.

There was an audible sigh of relief when the maids stepped back and the bullet puddings presented.

"Come now!" Beckoning them all to come forward, Lady Meyrick waved gently towards the bullet puddings. "But do be careful. I should not want anyone to jostle the table, at least not before the bullets have been placed there." Her gaze turned directly towards the Duke of Meyrick, who, seeing his mother's glance, nodded and quickly pulled two bullets from his pocket, having already been prepared, it seemed.

"To this table, gentleman," Lady Meyrick directed as her son carefully placed a bullet on top of the cake of flour. "And ladies to this table."

With a low groan, Jane made her way forward, catching Lord Northwick's grin as he passed towards her. He obviously had no qualms about playing this game.

"But perhaps he smiles because he wishes to be king," she muttered darkly to herself, looking around at all the other young ladies as they drew near. The older ladies in the house party – their mothers and chaperones – remained where they were, pushing their daughters forward. Indeed, as Jane looked about, her own mother had refused to come forward, but instead was speaking with Lady Renforth. They were talking and laughing about something and as Jane glanced back towards Lady Meyrick, she realized that nothing would be said about those who had chosen to remain absent from the table. It seemed this game was solely meant for unwed young ladies, as well as unattached gentlemen.

Her eyes closed briefly.

"I confess I feel a little unwell."

Jane squinted at her sister, who had come to stand beside her. "I am sure you need not be at all concerned. It is just a game." Speaking to herself as well as to Bettina, Jane drew in a steadying breath and clasped her hands in front of her. "If we concentrate, we will both do very well, I am sure."

Unfortunately, once the game had commenced, Jane quickly realized some of the ladies were being a good deal less careful than others. Some of them cut the cake with great enthusiasm, cutting out large chunks, while others shaved off only tiny pieces. Jane found herself holding her breath every time someone picked up the butter knife.

When it came to her turn, Jane took the knife quickly, hating the slight tremble in her fingers. Gritting her teeth, she sliced off a small section of the cake, and much to her relief, the bullet did not even wobble. Handing the knife over to the next lady, she waited with breathless anticipation, praying someone would make the bullet fall before her turn came around again. It was an entirely selfish desire, she knew, yet she simply could not bear to have to do such a thing again.

To her utter horror, however, the knife continued its travels around the group until there were only three others before her turn came again. The flour cake was getting ever smaller, and yet, the bullet still sat on top of it.

"Miss Ainsley?"

Bettina took the knife and sliced off a sliver before

setting it near to Jane. The silence in the room beat down upon her, tension making her fingers grip the knife hard as she grasped it. With a deep breath, she gritted her teeth and studied the flour cake. It was only one tall pillar now, with a bullet resting at the very top. She did not know where to cut, fearful the bullet would fall no matter what she did. Many of the young ladies around her were whispering and giggling now, seemingly delighted *they* would not have to do such a thing as this, clearly believing the bullet would fall very soon.

Swallowing hard, Jane drew in a breath, quickly ascertaining that no matter what she did, it would be luck as to whether or not she would succeed or fail. Taking the knife, she leaned forward a little and cut to the smallest slice she could from the flour cake. Her hand trembled as she did so, the tip of her knife touching the bullet and making it wobble. A little gasp of anticipation came from the ladies watching but, much to Jane's abject relief, the flour she had sliced away fell gently without cracking the remaining pillar of flour. Withdrawing the knife carefully, she still continued to grasp the handle, waiting for the bullet to decide her fate.

Much to her relief, it did not move. It did not roll to the side and fall, with a clatter, to the plate. Carefully setting the knife down beside next to her, Jane closed her eyes and allowed her tension to fade. She was safe now, surely? There would be no possibility of *her* face being pushed into the flour.

"Goodness." The murmur came from Miss Dyer as she reached to get the knife and Jane's heart twisted in sympathy for her. Just as the young woman made her cut, a great and explosive cheer came up from the gentlemen's table. Such was the sound that the poor lady jerked in surprise, the bullet was knocked and it fell to the plate. The sound ran around the room, and the young ladies at the table all began to laugh. Much to Jane's relief, however, Miss Dyer began to laugh also. When all the other ladies gathered around to press Miss Dyer's face into the flour, Jane herself stepped back, dropping her head and demanding her heart stop its frantic beating.

"Jane!" Bettina grasped her arm, her eyes vivid with excitement. "You have won!"

It took Jane a moment to understand what she meant. She had not lost the game, she realized, but she was now to be declared the Queen of the Christmas house party. After all, she had been the one standing next to Miss Dyer, had she not? Her dread returned, albeit not as strongly as before, and she dropped her head a little lower as everyone else in the room began to laugh, delighting in the two unfortunate souls whose faces were now very white indeed.

"Alas Miss Dyer and you too, Lord Winchester, you have both knocked the bullet and have dealt with the consequences of doing so... as we can all see!" Lady Meyrick laughed as the entire room erupted once more. Miss Dyer went across the room to stand beside Lord Winchester and together they faced the crowd, although Jane noted Miss Dyer was practically beaming in evident delight. Such a thing was a little unusual, was it not, given she had only just lost the game?

"Very well, very well," Lady Meyrick continued. "Then might I ask which of you gentlemen is to be declared our king?"

Jane looked around the room, twisting her fingers tight together as the gentleman glanced at each other, prolonging the moment. The tension grew, a great, thick cloud coming to hang over them all. While everyone else seemed to find it greatly amusing – for some were laughing and chortling – Jane herself was almost nauseated with the weight of it.

"Come now, gentlemen!" Lady Meyrick put both hands to her hips, clearly aware they were teasing her. "Is it to be my son, the Duke? Or you, Lord Stone? Or you, Lord Moorhead?"

"None of those, my lady."

To Jane's shock, none other than Lord Northwick raised his hand. Her eyes closed of their own accord as she realized she would have to spend one day and one night playing Queen, while Lord Northwick would play King. Yes, they were a little more amiable... but her concern was now that her strange feelings that came whenever he was near would grow in substance until she found herself all the more confused.

I wish I had taken my leave when I had the chance.

Seeing Bettina still near her, Jane grasped her hand quickly, intending to find a way to ask if her sister might take her place. She was prevented from saying even a single word to her, however, for Lady Meyrick then turned her attention to the ladies. Almost everyone pointed towards Jane and, thus, the deed was done.

With no smile on her face and a distinct heaviness over the acceptance of her current position, Jane dragged her feet as she came to stand beside Lord Northwick. He was grinning brightly, whereas she felt nothing but heaviness. But she could not escape it now. Jane was Queen of the Christmas party.

CHAPTER NINE

*L*ucius studied himself in the mirror, considering his somewhat altered appearance. He was wearing a long, dark red cape that fell almost to his ankles. His metal crown was dented and looked a little battered, making him wonder if Lady Meyrick had pulled it from a child's toy box! Regardless, it appeared as though he was going to have to wear it, and, along with the large staff topped with a decorative gold adornment, it was to be his costume for the rest of the evening and all of tomorrow.

Sighing, Lucius tipped his head, quietly thinking he looked quite the fool. No doubt it was part of the occasion, but for whatever reason, he was not at all in good spirits. Even though, when he had first realized he would be king, he had laughed uproariously.

Perhaps the reason for his gravitas was due to the look on Miss Ainsley's face when she discovered he was to be the King and she the Queen. There had not been any joy in her expression, but rather, her eyes had flashed, her lips going into a thin line as her shoulders dropped low. Everyone had laughed and cheered, but she had not even broken into a smile. He had every belief she was entirely disinclined to play the part of Queen and, he considered, if she could have given it to someone else, then no doubt she would have done!

"It seems as though, no matter what happens, we are going to be thrust together." Turning away from his reflection, he went from his room to the staircase, ready for the evening's entertainment to begin. Dinner had already been and gone, the port had been drunk and enjoyed... and then he had been told his costume was ready.

Taking a deep breath, he straightened his shoulders before he walked into the drawing room. The room suddenly broke into a great cheer and Lucius stopped dead, both surprise and embarrassment rippling up in his spine.

"Yes, yes. I look like a fool," he remarked, as Lord Renforth slapped him hard on the back. "But I believe since I am King, I can order you all not to allow yourself a single sound of mirth in my presence, is that not so?"

This did not have the effect he had hoped for. The gentlemen in the room once more broke into howls of laughter, clearly refusing to take his edicts with any seriousness.

"Ah, but Lord Northwick is quite correct!" Lady Meyrick rose from her seat, her arms spreading out wide above her head, as though she wanted to grasp the sound of the laughter and quell it. "You must do as he says! And if he says you are not to laugh, then..." She shrugged. "You are not to laugh." Her head turned at the sound of the door opening, and Lucius caught her broad smile. "And now, here comes the Queen to join the King."

A swell of anticipation rose and fell in his stomach as he turned, just as Miss Ainsley walked into the drawing room. She, too, had a cloak, but it was not red as his, but rather a dark, ivy green. Her red hair bore a silver crown, small and yet striking – a good deal better than his own – and the way she carried herself gave her an almost legal appearance. It was as if he ought to bow before her!

"Welcome your Queen." Clearly delighted with the play she was directing, Lady Meyrick gestured to him and, with a great deal of awkwardness given that every eye was on him, Lucius came near to Miss Ainsley, offering his arm and inclining his head as he did so. "Your Royal Highness."

With only a small smile, she set her hand on his arm, her eyes a little more rounded than they usually were. Her hand was cold as he reached to press it with his other, hoping it would be an encouragement.

"Your Majesty."

Her murmur was so quiet, Lucius barely heard it. However, there was not time for them to say anything more, for Lady Meyrick clicked her fingers, the door opened and the footmen brought in not one, but two very large wooden chairs, both seats covered in red velvet, with ornate decorations at the arms and along the back. Wherever they had come from, Lucius did not know, but it was clear these were meant to be thrones for himself and Miss Ainsley.

"We are to sit, I think." Muttering quietly to the lady, he led her forward as the chairs were set at one end of the room. Recalling he was to treat her as though she were the Queen, he set her in her chair first before turning to the crowd. With a smile, he took his staff, slammed it hard on the floor, and then sat down, keeping his back straight. Lady Meyrick clapped her hands, as did everyone else, and Lucius attempted to smile, fully aware of just how distinctly uncomfortable this entire façade was making him.

"With your humble permission, I should like to propose that the King issue his first declaration."

Lucius blinked, seeing Lady Meyrick's lifted eyebrow, but finding himself nonplussed.

"But first, let us all take our seats. The Duke will make certain anyone who wishes for a drink is offered one."

A little relieved he would have a few minutes to think, Lucius let out a slow breath, aware of the tightness in his chest. This was not in the least bit enjoyable.

"If you and I are playing at King and Queen, then might we not state there are to be no more parlor games for the duration of our reign?"

A little startled, Lucius turned his head and let out a chuckle, seeing the slight smile on Miss Ainsley's face, although her cheeks were still devoid of color. "You dislike this as much as I, I think." She nodded and, before he could prevent himself, he reached to cover her hand with his for just a few moments, while everyone else found their seats again, glass in hand. "The day shall be over very soon, I am sure, and then this nonsense will come to an end... for this evening, at least."

This gave him a small nod but nothing more, and they were left to look out at Lady Meyrick, who once more took charge of them all.

"We prepare for what task – or edict – the King and Queen shall set before us. Once you have completed what has been asked, the King and Queen will allow you respite until everyone has returned... and I am sure there will be consequences, or forfeits, for those who come last!"

A giggle came from a young lady and Lucius' stomach dropped. Whatever was he meant to say?

"I hope we shall have at least one this evening?"

The question from Lady Meyrick sent Lucius into something of a panic. He could think of nothing to entertain those present.

"My Queen?" Looking at Miss Ainsley with slightly widened eyes, he saw her smile and nod as relief ran like cool water through his frame. She herself had come up with an idea.

"You must all bring us some snow," she declared, her voice filling the room with a surprising amount of confidence. "You must not use any container, however. Whoever brings us the most shall win the round, but whoever brings us the least will have to accept a forfeit."

Lucius had not even noticed it had been snowing, but given the exclamations from others, it was obvious everybody else was already aware.

"Come there, prepare yourselves." Miss Ainsley rose to her feet, glancing back at him with a quick smile before she spread her arms out wide. "Recall: whoever returns with the largest amount of snow will be declared the winner, and whoever the smallest shall lose. Now go!"

With a great flurry of movement, the room erupted with squeals of excitement and a good deal of laughter from the gentleman. The last to quit the room were the older ladies and gentlemen amongst them, and Lucius heard one of them mutter something about the parlor, clearly unwilling to take part in the game. Very soon, all of the noise faded and, letting out a sigh, he slumped back in his chair, suddenly filled with appreciation for the young lady before him.

"You are exceptional, Miss Ainsley. I could think of nothing!"

When she sat down to face him, the last thing Lucius expected to see were flashing eyes that spoke of excitement. How different this was from the lady who had entered!

"I have had an idea."

"Indeed? Is this about more tasks and challenges for

them all? You will think me quite useless, since I can come up with nothing!" Sitting up a little straighter, he looked back at her expectantly.

"No, it is not about tasks. Well, I suppose it is, but not in the way you might expect." Taking a breath, she set her hand over his. "Why do we not ask them to write us a most gracious letter, expressing themselves to be our most willing, humble servants? Their platitudes and entries must be prepared by the morning, and you and I shall judge the greatest and the least from amongst them." Her face seemed to glow with anticipation, but Lucius could only frown.

"You wish to be serenaded? To be complemented?" This question brought nothing but laughter, and Lucius found himself smiling, even though he did not know what they were laughing about.

"No, indeed, I have a much better reason for suggesting such a thing."

Lucius jumped in shock as her fingers pressed through his, gripping his hand gently. "Would it not be a good opportunity to look at the handwriting of each and every person here? Of the *ladies* in particular?"

Lucius blinked, quickly realizing what she meant, as his astonishment turned to respect over her wisdom.

"Do you mean to compare each letter to the note I received?" A slight heat rose up in his chest as he recalled the first note. "I still have the first one I received on my dressing table that night."

This did not seem to bring her any surprise, for she merely nodded, her expression otherwise remaining the same. "Yes, comparing them is my intention. It might give you a hint as to who is responsible for writing such a thing."

Lucius shook his head, running one hand through his

hair. "My word, Miss Ainsley, you are a clever sort. It is an excellent idea."

A slight pink licked her cheeks, but her eyes remained fixed to his. Had they always been so vivid? So green? His chest tightened, his blood beginning to heat as he looked into her face, finding Miss Ainsley so incredibly beautiful – and not only that, but of an incredible character also.

"If we are to act this foolish part, then would it not be wise to use it to our own advantages?" Her voice had softened a little. "We would have enough time to compare them all come the morrow. Once we set yet *another* task for them – so everyone who has written a letter would be gone from the room, then we would be able to study each of the letters closely.

"Certainly it would be work," Lucius admitted, still marveling at her. "Very well. Once everyone returns with their snow, we shall declare the winner as well as those who must face the consequences! Thereafter, we direct them all to write this letter, which must be finished by the morning."

She nodded eagerly. "Precisely my thinking, Lord Northwick. I am so glad you agree."

His fingers tightened gently as he simply held her hand and looked into her eyes. It was very strange how they had gone from such fierce enemies to now, seeming to work together in an attempt to discover who had been writing him these notes. What made things all the more complicated was the fact his feelings for the lady were growing significantly – and in a direction he had never anticipated. Since there was now no particular difficulty between them, there came instead a gentle freedom to allow himself to feel whatever he wished. Except, as yet, he was not quite certain what it was he felt.

"Miss Ainsley." Not quite certain what it was he

wanted to say but finding he wanted to tell her something regardless, wanted to speak into the silence, Lucius drew in a breath. "I must tell you something. I have found myself –"

The door to the room was pushed back so hard that it flung back against the wall, making Miss Ainsley jerk furiously. His hand lifted from hers just as Miss Harding and Lord Rutledge came tearing into the room, hurrying to the table before setting down the block of snow they had each packed together, with the latter wringing his hands while Miss Harding ran to the fire to set her hands in front of it.

Finding himself frustrated that he was not to have any further time alone with Miss Ainsley, it took a moment for Lucius to smile.

"I can see you have both done very well." Miss Ainsley threw him a quick smile, then rose from her throne and approached the table. "We must have some measure by which we can judge just how much has been brought here." Looking back over her shoulder at Lucius, she arched an eyebrow and Lucius hurriedly removed himself from his seat, coming to join her.

"Yes, certainly we shall. I think –"

The door opened again as with two gentlemen and three ladies all coming in together. They were all laughing and casting glances over their shoulders – which Lucius could not comprehend until Lord Pendleton staggered into the room. He had taken the directive very seriously, for he had created blocks and blocks of compacted snow and then set them one atop the other, meaning he was carrying a very great amount! He walked with infinite slowness, the final block resting against his shoulder as though he were afraid he might drop it all at any given moment.

Lucius grinned. "My Queen, I believe we will have no need to judge anyone else's efforts!" he laughed, as the rest of the room exploded with mirth at the sight of Lord Pendleton attempting to set his snow down. "I would be very surprised indeed if anyone else is able to bring such an amount into the room!"

"I am very glad to hear it!" Lord Pendleton attempted, for the third time, to set his stack of snow down, only for one of the ladies to open a window wide and beg him to throw it back outside. Lucius gave his consent and Lord Pendleton, with some aid, removed his burden from himself, letting out a long breath of relief, his shirt rather damp.

"Thank goodness. I can barely feel my hands because it is so cold!

Lucius caught himself smiling, his gaze on Miss Ainsley, considering again just how beautiful she was. The fire lit her eyes, the smile she directed towards him making a fire light his own heart.

"All that is left is to declare who has lost," Miss Ainsley stated, turning her attention back to the room. "The rest of you shall have to place your attempts here on the table – and they are already melting, however, but –"

Her words were cut short by Lord Ossington, whom they had not noticed was yet absent. He walked in with his head low, snow lingering on his jacket, his knees and shirt appearing very wet indeed.

"I do not think you need to look any longer, Your Highness," he muttered, eliciting gasps of surprise and giggles of mirth at his appearance. "I have brought in very little snow because as I hurried up the stone steps, I tripped and my snow unfortunately fell from my hands... and decided to attach itself to my clothing." He brushed at it with his fingers. "I have only the smallest amount."

The dampness of his clothes and the mournful expression on his face had Lucius snorting with laughter, while

Miss Ainsley put one hand to her mouth to muffle the sound. Lord Ossington really was very wet indeed.

"Then I am afraid you have lost, Lord Ossington," Miss Ainsley declared, managing to control her laughter. "Although the tasks for this evening are not yet at an end! Mayhap you will be able to remedy matters."

Lord Ossington lifted his head, looking a little relieved. "There is to be another task?"

"The King and I have decided to set you all another task." Miss Ainsley explained quickly. "You must all write a letter to the King and to myself, giving your compliments and expressing yourself to be our most humble servants, in the very best way you can. Come the morrow, Lord Northwick – that is, the King and I – shall read them all and thereafter, decide who is the very best and the worst of them all." She grinned. "And so you see, Lord Ossington. This challenge will offer you the attempt to redeem yourself."

The gentleman bowed. "I shall go to write it at this very moment, my great and wonderful Majesty."

With a broad grin, Lord Ossington quickly turned and practically fled from the room, leaving everyone else to follow after him.

"We expect the very best of letters from all of you," Lucius declared, coming to stand beside Miss Ainsley. "They shall all be judged come the morning, so you have a good deal of time to pen your letter." Turning his head, he shared a smile with Miss Ainsley. "And then, mayhap, we shall learn who has been penning *particular* letters to me."

CHAPTER TEN

"Do we have any letters?"

Jane shivered lightly as Lord Northwick came to stand beside her as she sat at the dining table with many of the other guests. His nearness was not unexpected and yet it seems to bring about such a warmth within her that she could not explain it.

"I believe we have a letter from everyone, Lord Northwick.... or should I say, 'Your Highness'?" This last remark was said with a small smile, and Lord Northwick laughed engagingly as some of the other guests chuckled along with him.

"I believe we are still King and Queen for the remainder of the day," he remarked as she laughed lightly along with him. "So yes, Your Majesty, I inquire as to whether or not you have read any such letters as yet."

"I thought I would wait until you were present."

Lord Northwick smiled then and the light in his eyes seemed to speak of an appreciation for her consideration. "Then shall we begin, Miss Ainsley?"

A pile on the table beside her was her first consideration. The other guests had all arrived earlier that morning and had set their letters on the dining table near to her plate, but as yet she had not touched a single one of them. It had seemed wrong to do so, not when Lord Northwick had not been here with her. Now, however, she reached for the first one, only for the room to grow suddenly silent.

Lord Northwick looked up, his eyes going around the room as he grinned.

"Mayhap we should read them somewhere else, Your Majesty." Letting out a quiet laugh, he put one hand on her shoulder for a moment. "We shall find another place to read them, I think, away from prying eyes."

"I quite agree," she continued, making to rise from the table, only for him to settle one hand on her shoulder again, his fingers pressing lightly. "Please, do ensure you have broken your fast first. There is no particular rush as yet – although I suppose we must think of our eager subjects!" he finished, making Jane laugh. "They will think it's quite a torment, I am sure."

"But is not such a thing within the power of the King and Queen?" she responded, one eyebrow arching as a few giggles came from around the table. "I do believe you have not eaten anything yet either?"

"You are correct, I have not." With a grin, he gestured to the table. "Mayhap I shall sit for a short while."

Lady Meyrick rose from the table. "Please, eat!" She smiled in Lord Northwick's direction. "If your intention, Your Majesties, is to look over these letters in private, then might I suggest that those who await your judgment assist in the making of the *many* Christmas decorations for the Duke's house? We must also think of the greenery which must be brought in on Christmas Eve!"

Jane nodded. "Yes, I believe such a plan would be more

than suitable." She responded with as much confidence in her voice as she could manage. After all, if she was meant to be playing the part of a Queen, then it meant she would be higher in status than even Lady Meyrick, which, however, felt very disconcerting. Jane shied away from appearing so almost immediately. "Of course, only if you are quite contented to oversee such a thing, Lady Meyrick?"

She responded with alacrity. "I have prepared for such a situation, of course. You need to not have any concern, Your Majesties. I will have the guests continuing their task with the decorations until such a time as you are ready to see them again." She arched an eyebrow towards Lord Northwick. "I assume you will make quite certain there is a chaperone, however?"

A slight flush came to Jane's cheeks for, in the flurry of excitement over the situation, she herself had quite forgotten she would require someone else in the room with them. It was not as though she could be alone with Lord Northwick for a prolonged time.

No matter how much I seem to desire it.

Afraid her thoughts would reveal itself on her face, she dropped her head as Lord Northwick cleared his throat lightly.

"Yes, of course, Lady Meyrick. I shall have Lord Renforth with us." This was said with a quick glance, flinging itself towards the gentleman in question. To Jane's relief, the gentleman nodded immediately, although Jane did notice the flicker of surprise that lit the gentleman's eyes, finding herself grateful for his willingness.

"Excellent." Lady Meyrick smiled. "Once you are ready, I shall have a parlor prepared for you, perhaps with some more tea served in a short while, if you should like, Your Majesty?" This last part was directed to Jane, who nodded before returning her gaze to her breakfast plate. She was not particularly enjoying her role as Queen and was finding her nearness to Lord Northwick a good deal more unnerving than she had anticipated – although every time such a feeling came upon her, she cast it aside as quickly as she could. All she had to do was concentrate on the present task, especially since *she* was the one who had come up with the idea of a first place!

"I shall take these letters to the parlor." Lord Northwick smiled down at her. "I find I am not particularly hungry this morning. My appetite shall only be whetted by reading these letters!"

A murmur rang around the room as Jane quickly rose, not wishing to prolong the moment. "I am finished also. Shall we make our way to the parlor?"

"But of course." Lord Northwick agreed, just as Lord Renforth got to his feet also. "Pray excuse us."

After a moment, they were gone from the dining room and Jane's stomach began to swirl with a nervous anticipation.

"Alas, you shall have to read my letter also," Lord Renforth said heavily, unsuccessfully attempting to hide the grin spreading across his face as they made their way towards the parlor. "I confess it is not of any good standard."

Lord Northwick snorted as they made their way down the hall, offering her his arm as they went. She accepted it, trying to ignore the warmth beginning to pool in her stomach as she did so.

"The truth is, Renforth, we are not here to judge the letters," Lord Northwick explained as they stepped into the parlor. "We are here to determine who has written a letter to me."

"I beg your pardon?" Lord Renforth frowned; lines drawn over his forehead.

With a brief explanation, Lord Northwick settled Jane in a large, overstuffed chair near to the fire, while the letters were then deposited on the table.

"I see." Lord Renforth cleared his throat. "Then you will have to fetch that particular letter from your dressing table, will you not?"

"No. I have it already in my pocket." He took a breath, then gestured to the letters on the table. "Here, Miss Ainsley. If you would."

Jane licked her lips as Lord Northwick handed her the letter he had received at the first, their fingers touching for a moment. Immediately, butterflies began to beat their wings in her stomach as she unfolded it, almost afraid to discover what she would find written there.

"We should set the letters into two piles - those from gentleman and those from ladies." The letter slipping from her fingers as she fumbled with it.

"An excellent idea." Lord Renforth opened one, then set it down on the table. "This one was from Lord Rosenthal. Letters from gentlemen go here, and from the ladies shall go here." The two gentlemen busied themselves with unfolding letters and determining whether or not each one had been written by a gentleman or lady, while Jane herself unfolded the note Lord Northwick had given her. She did not need to read it, of course, but somehow could not prevent her eyes from roving over it. As she did so, however, she found herself blushing furiously. The letter was clear in its intentions to Lord Northwick, offering eager and intentional encouragements – something Jane herself would *never* have written!

"I believe we have all the letters from the ladies here."

Lord Northwick gestured to a small pile to one side of the table. "And you have Lord Northwick's letter still, Miss Ainsley?"

Jane nodded, licking her dry lips. "Yes. It is here." Rising from the chair, she came to join them, spreading it out between the two piles. Lord Northwick picked up one of the letters from the ladies, then spread it out beside the first. They looked for a long moment at the sloping letters of the first letter and the slightly taller letters from the second and all expressed disagreement at the very same time.

"No, I do not think so." Jane shook her head. "See how these letters are written? They appear so very different."

"There is always the possibility that the person who wrote the first note may have disguised their handwriting in some way." The suggestion from Lord Northwick was not a welcome point, for it made Jane's spirits drop a little.

"I am certain we will find some similarity soon," she murmured, half to herself, half to encourage herself. "We *must*."

Some thirty minutes later, Lord Renforth set down the last letter and then settled back in her chair with a sigh. The promised tea had not yet arrived as yet and Jane felt parched, even though it has only been a short while – less than an hour since she had broken her fast.

"I do not understand it." Shaking his head, Lord North-wick gestured to all of the notes. "It seems as though *none* of these match the note I was given."

Lord Renforth shook his head. "We have looked through all of them, have we not? Sharing them out so we made our way through them." Gesturing to the letters, he threw up both hands. "Perhaps it is as I have said – the person who has written this note does not *want* to be found.

Mayhap they are wily, aware you might attempt to do such a thing. Perhaps we have underestimated them."

Taking a deep breath, Jane set her shoulders, determined not to give up. "Let us look at *all* the letters," she suggested quietly. "Thus far, we have taken one each and compared them. Instead, let us take one at a time, and, with great care, look at it. I shall look at it, and you, Lord Renforth, and then you also, Lord Northwick. Mayhap it will be one of us sees something the others do not. The letter does not have to be exactly the same, but there should be some similarities." She looked from one gentleman to the other, but only Lord Northwick nodded. Lord Renforth sighed, his jaw tight. Perhaps believed it was already a lost cause.

"At least, then, we shall be thorough." With a quick smile in her direction, Lord Northwick picked up the first letter, and Jane could not help but watch him as he looked from one to the other, comparing the first to the second. She caught the way his eyes flashed, his gaze focused with purpose. Would he ever look at her with such intention?

Giving herself a small shake to push such thoughts away, Jane took the note from him, catching the slight shake of his head. She studied it closely for some moments, but thereafter accepted immediate instinct that this letter was not the same as the note he had received. The letters were far too slanted. She handed it to Lord Renforth for his opinion, just as Lord Northwick picked up the second. This went on for some time, and Jane soon found her heart beginning to sink. There did not seem to be a single letter that matched the note he had discovered. What were they to do? This grand plan of hers had seemed a great one, and she had been very sure indeed they would be able to find a clue, at least, as to who might have written this letter but now it did not appear so easy.

"Wait a moment." Lord Northwick nudged her lightly. "It is not exactly the same, but perhaps...?"

The letter was handed to Jane, and she began to read the first few lines. Stopping abruptly, she then compared them to the note Lord Northwick had set out. Holding one beside the other, she compared the handwriting, realizing there certainly were some similarities. There were not a good many of them, but there were some.

"It is a possibility, certainly," she murmured, handing them both to Lord Renforth for his opinion. "Some of the letters appear to be formed in the same way, I think."

"They are not exact, however." Taking the letter back from Lord Renforth, Lord Northwick seemed to avoid her gaze. "We may still be correct in our assessment, however."

"It is the first one that has appeared similar in any way, similar, so surely we must give ourselves a little hope!"

Lord Northwick cleared to throat, his gaze flicking to hers but not quite catching her eyes. "Yes, of course, but it is only to say –"

"I quite agree." Lord Renforth interrupted, taking the letter from in Lord Northwick's hand and beginning to unfold it. "I believe I was the one who looked at this the first time around. I am sorry I did not notice the similarities before." He turned smiling eyes to Jane. "I think your suggestion has proven to have been an excellent one. It seems we may have found our culprit!"

"Let us not be too hasty." Much to Jane's surprise, Lord Northwick reached out and took the letter from Lord Renforth's fingers so quickly that it made a gentle snapping sound. "We may be mistaken. There are only *some* similarities."

"But given there are no connections between any of the other letters, then surely we must –"

"We need to finish looking at the rest of the letters before we can make that sort of distinction." Lord Northwick folded up the letter and placed it in his pocket. Jane followed his actions with her eyes, wondering why he was doing such a thing. Was there something he wished to keep from both herself and Lord Renforth?

Lord Renforth shrugged. "Then let us go through the rest of the letters." Picking up another, he unfolded it quickly, clearly less concerned as to why Lord Northwick was behaving in such a manner. Silence flooded the room as they began to sort through the rest of the letters. Jane did her best to study each and every one but could not find similarities in any of them. Lord Northwick's figure seemed to grow a little more hunched as he looked through them, one after the other. It was as though he were twisting in on himself, his shoulders pulling towards his ears, his back rounding in a little more. There was a heavy frown on his face that dropped his eyebrows low, and the intensity of his gaze spoke of a great deliberation. It was obvious he was taking great lengths to study each letter but, as yet, had found nothing that would be of aid to them. It seemed the single note they had discovered was in fact the one they required, but why he had slipped it into his pocket, she did not know.

"There, you see?" Lord Renforth grinned with obvious delight. "There is no other. The one we have discovered is the correct one."

"I believe Lord Renforth is correct." Turning careful eyes towards Lord Northwick, Jane watched his frown darken even more. Why was he responding so? She had thought he would be pleased; glad now they had found the correct one. What was it about it that displeased him so? Perhaps, she considered, he had been hopeful the letter had been from Lady Borthwick, and now that it was not, he found himself severely disappointed.

Lord Northwick's frown remained as he glanced at her. "We are also to determine a winner of these letters. Miss Ainsley. Have you any of particular note? Mayhap if you would, you could set it aside? Lord Renforth, might I have a word?"

Jane found herself moving a little closer to Lord Northwick, her brows dropping in frustration. "I confess I am all too aware of your attempts to push me from the present conversation." Her quiet statement had Lord Northwick glancing at her again as Lord Renforth remained where he was. "You are keeping me from this matter, are you not? I do not understand why you do so. After all, is it not *I* who stated I wished to aid you with this?"

"Yes, you did." Even though Lord Northwick directed his attention towards her, his gaze did not linger, drifting to somewhere over her shoulder. "But I can take the matter forward from here. There is no need for you to involve yourself any further." He gave her a soft smile, which did not bring any light to his eyes, and it faded so quickly that Jane knew instantly it had been forced. "Besides, I am certain a young lady such as yourself has a good deal more to do than aid me in my search for whoever has written me such foolish letters as these."

The thought that planted itself in Jane's mind grew with such ferocity she could barely contain her shock. She moved back suddenly, bumping into a chair which scraped violently on the floor. She stumbled against it, her eyes widening as both Lord Northwick and Lord Renforth stepped forward, but Jane simply shook her head, her hand held out towards Lord Northwick, one finger pointing. "You do not wish me to know because you intend to pursue this, do you not?" Her heart was suddenly pounding furiously, her stomach churning so violently she felt as though she might cast up her accounts at any moment. For whatever reason, the thought of Lord Northwick being close to any particular lady was making her heart tear itself into pieces, sending hot tears into the edges of her eyes.

"No."

Lord Northwick shook his head. "I can assure you it is not for that reason." Taking another step closer to her, he spread out his hands. "I assure you, I have no intention of seeking out this lady and accepting what she offers me."

Her vision blurred, tears threatened to run down her cheeks. She did not think she felt this strongly for Lord Northwick, but now it seemed she was almost ready to *cry* over him, which was most unlike her.

"Then why do you not tell me?" She used all of her inner strength to lift her head until they were simply looking back into each other's eyes. "You say you have had enough from me, but I do not understand why."

As the strength in her words grew, it was as if there were only the two of them in the room, for Lord Renforth's presence seemed to fade away. Her eyes flared in astonishment as Lord Northwick suddenly stepped towards her, his hand warm as it took hers, a fervency lighting his hazel eyes. Her tears faded, her pulse quickening suddenly at his nearness.

"Because I must be sure." The steadiness in his gaze and the press of his hand made her heart throw itself from one side of her chest to the other and she could not utter a single word.

"If I am wrong – if *we* are wrong, then I will have given

her name to both yourself, Miss Ainsley, and also to Lord Renforth. If the lady is entirely innocent, then I do not feel as though it would be right to give you her name until I am entirely certain of it." He dropped his gaze for a moment, chewing the edge of his lip. "What do *you* think?"

Jane silently berated herself for not unfolding the letter fully and reading the name at the bottom. Her desire to know, to understand exactly why Lord Northwick was hiding the name from her grew steadily, and yet his response to her begged her quietly to trust him.

Sighing, she looked back at him. "I think I wish there was a way to discern whether or not you speak the truth."

Lord Northwick shuffled his feet, moving a little closer in the process, his lips twisting. "I understand it is difficult for you to believe my words; to accept I am telling you what is true, but I assure you every word comes with honesty." He was so close to her now that the very air he breathed brushed across her cheek, firing such a response within her, she forgot completely about Lord Renforth's presence and even of what they were discussing, finding her breath shuddering out from her as she looked into his face.

"I must know the truth before I reveal it," he continued, speaking in a soft tone that seemed to soothe her fractious worries. "I do not want to injure you – or anyone else – unnecessarily."

Jane wanted to express a response to this, but her words simply would not come. There was something about this closeness, this nearness to him had all sense fading from her. Her silence must have concerned Lord Northwick, mayhap appearing as though she did not believe him, for he sighed and looked away, rubbing his free hand over his chin, to her surprise, taking her other hand also.

She had never been this close to a gentleman before. It

was unnerving but also so very, very wonderful.

"Would that I had a pristine reputation." His smile was a little sad as Jane swallowed against the constriction in her throat, struggling to hear him over the pounding of her heart in her ears. "Everything I thought had merit I would have given up, had I known I would have to fight for your belief in my character."

"Do I truly mean that much to you?"

The words came from her mouth before she could prevent them, and despite the warmth blossoming in her cheeks, Jane awaited his response without speaking another word. The steadiness in Lord Northwick's contemplation was as unyielding as before. There was no flicker of amusement in his dark eyes, and as he held both of her hands, Jane found her heart beating with a great urgency, desperate to know what it was he would say.

"Yes."

She closed her eyes briefly.

"I find your consideration of my character is one of the only things concerning me of late. I think of it almost every hour, wishing I had the power to change it."

The strength of his words pelted against her heart, chasing every last lingering bit of doubt from her. She no longer thought he was keeping this name from her because of his own desire to follow after the lady. The firmness of his expression and the fervency of his words told her otherwise.

And could that mean there is more in his heart for me than a desire for a better acquaintance?

The question brought such an overwhelming heat with it that Jane forced her gaze away, quite certain that Lord Northwick could feel it in her hands, if not see it in her face. She dared not to look at him and it was only when he spoke her name in quiet tones that she finally lifted her eyes to his again.

"I swear that I shall give you the name as soon as I am able, *if* it proves to be viable." Sets of lines drew themselves across his forehead, clearly still concerned that he would not be believed. "I assure you, I will do so."

Taking in a breath, Jane's fingers curled a little more tightly around his. "I believe you."

The change in his expression was so immediate, Jane was caught somewhere between laughter and embarrassment. His eyes widened, the lines of worry scurrying away, and his mouth fell a little ajar. After a moment, he bowed his head, letting out an audible breath that had his shoulders rounding.

His relief was so apparent that Jane felt the desire to comfort him a little more. Her hand lifted from his, and with a brief hesitation, came to settle on his shoulder. "I... I am sorry."

Lord Northwick lifted his head sharply. "There is nothing for you to apologize for.

"I believe there is." Her heart was beating so furiously, blood roaring in her ears, so she could hardly hear herself speak. "I should not have suggested you wished to take advantage of the situation for yourself. I am sorry."

Lord Northwick smiled, his eyes dancing about her face and his hand dropping to the curve of her waist. Jane drew in such a sharp breath that Lord Northwick immediately stepped back, his hands lifting slightly as hers swung back to her side. They simply looked at each other for a long moment, with Jane overwhelmed by how near he had been to her and how much she had wanted him to draw still closer. These desires were none she had ever experienced before, and the strength of them was extraordinary.

The door opened and Jane turned to it with a gasp of surprise, only for Lord Renforth to lift an eyebrow in her direction. He had evidently stepped outside for a moment, although she had not noticed his departure.

"I thought you might require a few moments of privacy."

Her face burned as she looked away, praying her reputation was not damaged in any way.

"I was only just outside the door." Lord Renforth spoke quickly, as though he could read Jane's fears. "Are you at an end of your conversation now?"

"We are." Lord Northwick cleared his throat abruptly, making Jane start. "Although we have not decided which letter is to be declared the winner and which the very worst."

Jane pressed one hand to her forehead, surprised at how much she was shaking. "I – I need to take a few moments respite." Not looking at either gentleman, she waved her hand in the direction of Lord Northwick. "Pray decide such things for yourself. I will join you within the hour back in the drawing room."

He came closer to her but Jane drew away. "Are you quite well, Miss Ainsley?"

She did not even look at him as he spoke, hurrying to the door for fear her expression would give her away. "Yes, perfectly well but a little fatigued. Do excuse me."

It was with relief Jane pulled the door shut behind her. What would have happened if Lord Renforth had seen her and Lord Northwick in what had practically been an embrace? And why was it the more she hurried away from the room, the more her heart yearned to go back directly into Lord Northwick's arms?

CHAPTER ELEVEN

"I would advise you to be careful, but I believe my words would be wasted, given you must surely already know to be cautious."

Lucius let out a long breath. "Yes, you have no need to tell me. I am already very well aware I should be prudent in this regard." Rubbing one hand over his face, all too aware of the lingering heat in his frame, he let out another heavy breath. "I did not mean to draw as close to her as I did."

"Be glad I did not see," came his friend's reply. "Else, if I had, I am sure I would have been very cross with you indeed." Lord Renforth's eyebrows lifted. "After all, I am here to make certain Miss Ainsley's reputation was protected."

Lucius resisted the groan in frustration. He had never expected to find himself so close to Miss Ainsley, especially not when they had been arguing only a few moments before. He had been hurt by her accusation, but in the moments thereafter had seen her soften and had found his heart softening with it. He had taken her hand on instinct, intending to drop it, only for her to move closer. When she had set her hand on his shoulder, his whole body had burned with a furious fire, sweeping through it with great strength, and he had been forced to use every modicum of his self-control to remain exactly where he was. His strength had broken as he had dropped his hand to her waist, and it had only been the presence of Lord Renforth that had pushed them apart. What exactly would he have done if Lord Renforth not stepped into the room? Would he have kissed her? That had been the desire in his heart, had it not? It was what he had wanted to do... and still did.

"You would not tell her who signed the letter." The statement was said with curiosity at the edge of it, and Lucius only nodded. The truth was, what he had discovered was so very shocking, he was afraid to mention it – even to Lord Renforth.

"You will not say a word to me about it either, it seems." Lord Renforth held up both hands. "Very well, I shall not press you. This must be very grave if you are being this evasive."

"Yes, it is very serious." The shock of it was still so great, Lucius could not quite take it in. "At this time, I am struggling to believe the sight of my own eyes!"

Lord Renforth's eyes widened as he took in a sharp breath. "Wait a moment! Does this mean the lady who has been sending you these notes is already wed?" He took a step closer, his voice dropping to a hushed tone. "Is that why you do not wish anyone to know her name?"

Lucius shook his head. "No, she is not wed." The heaviness of what he had learned sat heavily on his shoulders, and after a moment of consideration, Lucius set his shoulders and lifted his chin. "Whether or not this *is*, in fact, the person responsible, I should not like to make any accusations or the like until we can be quite sure." With a small smile, he looked directly at his friend. "Where are the ladies at present?"

"They are all making Christmas decorations at the King and Queen's request, if you recall." Lord Renforth answered, a slight glint to his eye. "What is it you intend to do? How is it you will prove this?"

Lucius did not answer. Ideas were floating through him, one after the other, but fading quickly as holes appeared in all of them in turn. With a long breath, he shook his head. "I am not sure as yet. I must be careful. This could prove very serious indeed."

"If there is anything I can do, you need only ask." Making his way to the door, Lord Renforth gestured to it, and after a moment Lucius stepped out, with his friend following after.

"I appreciate that, Renforth." Lucius grimaced, his mind still quarrelling over Lord Renforth's last question. How was he to prove who the bearer of the letter was? As yet, he could not think of a single idea, but his instinct told him to keep it from Miss Ainsley for as long as he could. To tell her would only distress her greatly, and given he had done a lot to injure her already, he did not want to even add more to her shoulders.

"The King has returned." Lady Meyrick looked up from the table as all the young ladies in the room fell silent, the tables they sat by filled with all kinds of greenery, unlit candles, twine and different colors of paper. All eyes were all fixed to Lucius, their hands stilling as though he were about to declare the winner of the letters at this very moment.

"I am afraid I can tell you nothing, not until my Queen arrives," Lucius said grandly, immediately eliciting a few murmurs of disappointment from those sitting near to him.

"And of course, the gentleman will need to be present also."

"Then perhaps you should like to make the announcement during luncheon," Lady Meyrick suggested, as Lucius nodded. "Might I ask where the Queen is?"

Lucius was about to say she had gone to rest for a short while, only for her voice to float near to him.

"The Queen is here."

Lucius turned just as she took his arm, her fingers rather tight. Lucius' eyebrows lifted, a little surprised at how strongly she held to him. It was almost as if she required his strength simply just to stand tall. Was she still overly tired after reading those letters and comparing them all?

"Miss Ainsley," he murmured. "Lady Meyrick has suggested we keep our counsel at present and declare the winner of the letters to our subjects over luncheon." His eyes searched her face, but she did not look directly back at him. "Does that suit you well enough?"

"But of course."

To Lucius' eyes, Miss Ainsley appeared a little distracted, although given what they had discussed, he could not blame her for it. Indeed, she must surely be feeling a little irritated he knew the name of the person he believed to be responsible, but she did not. Was that why she clung to his arm so tightly? Was that why her gaze jumped from one person to the other, her face now a little paler than before? Perhaps it was frustration rather than anything else.

"It shall be luncheon in a short while." Lady Meyrick spoke to the ladies at the table rather than to Miss Ainsley and Lucius. "Might you wish to join us, Your Majesty? I am sure the King will wish to go in search of the gentlemen wherever they may be."

Glancing at Miss Ainsley, Lucius was somewhat taken aback when her eyes flashed to him with the slight widening there also. Was she trying to communicate something to him? It was gone in a second with Miss Ainsley assenting quickly, for even though they played Kings and Queens at the present moment, no one could refuse the mother of a Duke.

"I should be glad to, Lady Meyrick." Her eyes went to his again. "Mayhap you and I might speak a little later, so we might decide what our task is to be for our subjects this afternoon?"

"Certainly." Lucius continued to hold her gaze for a few moments before she was forced to join the other ladies. Both he and Lord Renforth turned on their heels and made their way from the room, going in search of the other gentlemen as Lady Meyrick had suggested.

"I do hope Miss Ainsley is not too overcome by all of this." Lord Renforth rubbed at his chin. "She did not appear entirely herself to my eyes – a little white in the face, I think."

"Yes, I thought so too," Lucius mused, walking slowly along the hallway. "I did wonder if perhaps she might be a little frustrated with me, since I have not told her the name of the person I believe to be responsible." That consideration began to shrink back as he recalled the way her hand had pressed to his arm and the obvious flash in her eyes when they had been separated. Something more was unsettling her.

"I think I shall take a few moments in my bedchamber." he murmured, feeling the need to suddenly absent himself from all company. "I do hope you will excuse me."

"But of course," Lord Renforth agreed quickly, considering him. "You are well, I hope?"

"Yes, yes, quite well. I require a few moments of peace, nothing more." Lucius lifted one hand and then turned away, hurrying to the staircase so he might to walk along the hallway to his bedchamber, much like Miss Ainsley herself had done. His thoughts were heavy, his heart sinking as he thought about the name he now had in his mind and what he was to do next. He could come up with no easy answer and the name itself was giving him great cause for concern.

"I may be wrong." Muttering to himself, Lucius pushed one hand through his hair before rubbing it across his eyes. "I *must* be mistaken."

Walking into his bedchamber, Lucius made his way to a chair by the still-warm coals glowing gently in the grate, only to come to a sudden stop. There was something placed on his bed, something that certainly was not his. Yet again, someone had either been in his bedchamber or had sent their maid to do it, for there, resting gently at the head of his bed directly on the pillow, was a single rose. Tied with a purple ribbon, another note lay alongside it.

With deep breath. Lucius made his way towards it, picking up the note and ignoring the red rose. Whoever it was had taken clear advantage of the fact he was not present in his room. Part of him wanted to throw the note into the embers and see it alight, but instead he forced himself to read through the lines.

'You must forgive me for not coming to the library. I saw you were accompanied by another gentleman, therefore did not wish to reveal myself to you both. My affections are for you only. Did you fear it was some sort of trap? Did you fear mockery? Indeed, I assure you my eagerness for your closeness is just as it seems. I should never trick you into anything and have no desire to mock you. My only hope is that soon, our warm and pleasant company might begin.'

There was not even a question about whether or not Lucius himself desired such company. Evidently, the writer believed he would *always* avail himself of such a thing whenever it was offered and such a thing was to his shame. He did not *want* to have such a reputation. Ever since he had met Miss Ainsley here at the house party, his desires had changed significantly. He had been genuine when he had spoken of his eagerness to only be in Miss Ainsley's company, to think only of her consideration of him. Even now, it was the only thing that mattered.

His gaze returned to the letter, forcing himself to read the last few lines.

'If you desire to be as close to me as I might be to you, then come to the arbor this evening, some two hours after the festivities have begun, so I might know you are as eager to share closeness as I am to offer it. Show me whether or not my company is desired by coming to find me, in the cold winter night so our close connection might commence. I shall be waiting.'

Lucius pinched the bridge of his nose, a deep breath rattling out of him. The final few lines were full of hope and promise, but Lucius had no desire to take a hold of anything this lady was offering him.

"But I must pretend otherwise."

It felt wrong even to *consider* doing as the lady in this letter asked of him – but he had no other choice. He would have to go to the arbor, meet the lady and, thereafter, confront her.

Should I tell Miss Ainsley of this?

He shook his head, his first instinct being no, only to then reconsider. He could tell her of the note without being specific, for he did not want to keep anything from her, not if he did not have to.

"But what happens if it is as I fear?"

He could barely give his fear a voice such was the severity of consequences that would follow, should it be so. Fear coiled itself around his limbs, a deep and dreadful worry that he would have no other choice but to step away from Miss Ainsley for good. Something had happened between them, something he could not give name to nor could explain, but yet felt deep within himself.

Taking a deep breath, he straightened, standing tall. Yes, he would have to speak to Miss Ainsley about the matter and yes, he would have to tell her the truth about this note, but while doing so, he would keep the name of the lady he thought responsible entirely to himself. It was the *only* way he could continue on with this plan, and the only way he could keep Miss Ainsley close.... although Lucius could foresee a time when she would be the one to push him further away than he had ever been before.

CHAPTER TWELVE

The nausea swirling around Jane's stomach did not leave her for the remainder of the day. It lingered there every time she thought about the two notes she had compared. In her mind, over and over again, she saw the similarities between the letters and felt the same strange sense of awareness still within her.

The morning had passed in something of a blur. She had sat with the ladies as they had continued to make decorations for the Duke's house, had smiled as best she could and had taken part in conversation where she was able. At the same time, however, her mind had not been a part of it. It was still on those letters, still afraid to accept what she feared was the truth.

Luncheon had been a most merry affair, but she had fought to enjoy even a moment of it. Moreover, Jane had been unable to think of a single task for the guests, and it had fallen to Lord Northwick to do so. He had declared the winner of the letters as well as loser - although Jane herself had no particular interest in either – and had then stated they would all take a brisk afternoon walk out in the snow before dinner and the evening's entertainments. Quite what it was they were to be offered by way of such entertainment, Jane was not yet sure, but Lady Meyrick had promised a very special evening, with some of it to be spent out of doors.

Lord Northwick had not approached her during their walk as yet. It was very cold indeed, but Jane did not notice the chill, absently watching the flakes of snow that fell lightly around them. The rest of the house party seemed to be in very high spirits, with most of the older gentlemen and ladies choosing to stay indoors, although no doubt they watched them from the windows – Jane's own mother included. Glancing towards the gentleman in question, seeing how he walked alongside Lady Renforth, Jane looked away again sharply. Lord Northwick was laughing at something he had said to her, and Jane's stomach twisted suddenly. It was not as though she had anything to be concerned with over Lady Renforth's company, but more that she wished Lord Northwick might pay *her* the same attentions, so she might be pulled from this deep and unsettling melancholy.

Or perhaps it is that I want him to tell me the name on the letter, so I might be certain of what I fear.

Her attention suddenly dropped away from Lord Northwick, going back to the letter once more. If Lord Northwick did not want to tell her the truth about the letters, it could be for the reasons he said, or it could be for another reason entirely... one she was very fearful of indeed. He was trying to protect her, yes, but protecting her from the truth for fear it would cause her pain was no aid at all, especially when such a pain was already beginning to push into her heart.

"It is cold, is it not?"

Her sister linked her arm through Jane's, laughing at Jane's startled expression. "I myself am quite glad of it, I think. I do rather enjoy a winter walk, albeit not for too long." Her smile faded a little. "Those grey clouds look rather ominous."

Jane made some vague murmur of interest but said nothing in particular. Bettina frowned, looking back at Jane before setting her eyes to the skies again. "I do think you need not be anxious," she continued, clearly taking Jane's quiet mood for concern. "I am certain it will pass by the evening."

"Let us hope so." Jane glanced at her sister, then pulled it away again. "I do wonder what it is Lady Meyrick has planned for us. She asked my permission, of course, given that I am to be the Queen for the evening. But it was clear it was already planned so it was not as though I could refuse!"

Her sister laughed. "This has all been some great play on her part." She shook her head, chuckling again. "I think she has enjoyed it more than anyone else! I am sorry if your role does not put you in very best of spirits this afternoon. Are you quite well?"

"I am well enough." Jane did not give the truth to her sister, keeping it back. Bettina nodded slowly, as though somehow she understood. The tightness in Jane's throat grew, and she swallowed quickly, pushing it away and praying her sister would not prolong such a conversation.

"It must be very trying to realize you are beginning to like the very gentleman you have been trying to push away."

Jane almost stumbled as she swung her gaze directly back to her sister, her breath catching tightly in her chest. Bettina looked back at her for a moment, then shrugged her shoulders. "You do not think it has gone unnoticed, do you?" she asked quietly. "I am your sister. Of *course* I have noticed the amount of time you have spent with Lord Northwick, as well as the many glances you sent in his direction and the color that comes into your cheeks whenever there is as much as a mere mention of him – much as there is now."

Resisting the urge to press her hands to her face in order to cool her heated cheeks, Jane satisfied herself with a small shrug. Bettina, however, only laughed – a laugh which sounded a little strained and, to Jane's frustration, unsettled her all the more.

"You do not intend to tell me you have no interest in Lord Northwick, surely?"

Jane sighed and threw her sister a look, only for Bettina's eyebrows to lift.

"You *are* to pretend otherwise." There came a moment's pause. "Perhaps that is for the best. I do not think Lord Northwick is a gentleman suited to you, given his reputation."

Jane hesitated before she replied. Had she truly been so obvious? Her growing interest in Lord Northwick was something she had not yet even *admitted* to herself as yet! All the same, the urge to defend him grew swiftly.

"I know I have spoken badly of him for some time, Bettina, but I do not think his reputation of being a rogue is a fair one," she stated, desiring to put across a fair opinion. "He has certainly done a few things that might cause him to be considered by some to be a rascal, mayhap, but I think calling him a scoundrel is going too far."

Bettina smiled back, although something flashed in her eyes. "Never did I think my sister would be the one to defend Lord Northwick to me," she murmured softly, as Jane kept her eyes steadfastly away. "You *have* changed in your opinion of him."

"Our acquaintance has grown to a friendship, I will admit," Jane replied. "Nothing more, of course, for there is still restraint to be had there, but I was wrong to be so very harsh towards him. I want you to know of my change of mind in this."

"I confess I am glad to hear your honest words," Bettina replied, a little more sharply than Jane had expected. "Although I have every belief, you will continue to be cautious around him. You have always been wise in your choice of companions. I am glad to see such wisdom has not failed yet."

Jane did not know what to say, struggling for her response. Her sister, she reminded herself, did not know Lord Northwick particularly well. She had only heard Jane repeatedly berate him and almost constantly warn her away from being in his company. She could not expect Bettina to think anything else now.

Unless, of course...

"I am so excited about this evening's entertainment!" Another one of the guests, Miss Harding, came immediately to fall into step beside Bettina and Jane, interrupting their conversation. "Have you heard what it is going to be? Lady Meyrick apparently let slip to one of the other ladies during the Christmas decorations."

"No, we have not," Bettina replied, now reaching for Miss Harding's arm instead of Jane's. "Do tell us!"

Miss Harding giggled. "Apparently, it is to be a grand winter party. There will be a great many fires and I believe even fireworks in the night sky! There will be refreshments and hot cocoa out of doors and while we shall all have to dress up warm, there will be food and the like served indoors also, if we become too chilled. I believe there will be all sorts of entertainments outside, however she was not specific as to what they would be. I confess myself to be very excited!" She giggled again, and the sound set Jane's teeth on edge, going against everything she was currently battling with inwardly. It was not as though she could think of enjoyment and entertainment when she was so very troubled over these letters and, indeed, Lord Northwick.

Miss Harding's voice dropped low. "I have no doubt there will be plenty of dark places... shadows where we might hide ourselves away for a particular gentleman to come and steal his forfeit. I do not think we shall be carefully chaperoned tonight."

This thought brought no pleasure to Jane, and she tensed, her fingers stretching out wide before curling into tight fists. Bettina, on the other hand, fell into giggles with Miss Harding while Jane slowed her steps, allowing the two ladies to go ahead of her. Her heart was fearful, fearful for her sister and what difficulty she might fall into, should what Jane believed be revealed as the truth.

"Miss Ainsley?"

Her head turned, her heart caught. Lord Northwick stood beside her, having obviously been watching her, aware she now stood as the last of the group, lost in her own thoughts. The urge to fling herself into his arms began to sear through her and, astonished at her own boldness, Jane grasped his hand and tugged him a little ways behind a tree.

Lord Northwick's eyes flared immediately, but Jane did not hold back. Her hand was tight on his, her eyes searching his face. "I cannot wait another moment." Her gaze fixed as he pressed back against the tree, the air between them foggy with the heat of their breath. "The note you found. The note we realized was similar to the one you had received." Swallowing hard, she closed her eyes, suddenly afraid of the answer but yet demanding silently she speak, regardless. "It - it was from my sister, was it not?"

Her only answer was silence. Her chest was heaving, as though someone had wrapped their arms tight around her, holding her fast. It was not a pleasant sensation, however, and she could only take in shallow breaths. It was only when he said her name gently, she finally dared to open her eyes.

"Why do you ask me this?" Lord Northwick's voice was pained, as though this was something he did not want to tell her. "I swore I would not tell you until I learned the truth."

"Yet I must know." She looked back into his face, her hands still tight around his as though just by her presence, she could convince him of her earnestness. "I am so very afraid and yet the truth seems to be snaking around me, no matter how much I try to avoid it."

Lord Northwick sighed, his eyes closing briefly. "I cannot be sure of anything, Miss Ainsley."

Letting out a shuddering breath, Jane moved even closer. "But you saw similarities between her note and the note you received that night."

"As did you," he answered gently. "Yet you did not see her name – I am aware you will know your sister's hand, but it was obviously not immediately obvious to you. What is it now that makes you fear *she* wrote to me?"

It was as though her world were slowly collapsing in on her. "I realized something." Her voice was trembling, and if Lord Northwick had not been holding her hand carefully, then she was quite certain her hands would be shaking too. "When I spoke to her about the note – the one with our name on it, the one slipped into your pocket at the ball, I spoke to her of my concern, to make certain she knew of the situation and was not worried." Her eyes grew hot with tears. "She mentioned the library."

Lord Northwick nodded slowly, clearly not understanding. Jane, to her embarrassment, became aware of gentle tears falling to her cheeks. "I did not ever mention the library to her, Lord Northwick. I only became aware of her slip when I read the notes with you and Lord Renforth this afternoon."

"Which was why you had to take your leave."

She nodded, unable to say anything for a few moments, such was the agony in her throat. The long breath that came from Lord Northwick told her of his shock and, along with it, the realization she was not alone in her belief that Bettina was the one who had been writing such notes.

A groan came from her, and she dropped her head. "I fear I have been wrong from the beginning. I am afraid that, during the masquerade ball last Season, my sister *intended* for you to pull her away. Had I not intervened, then she would have willingly gone into your arms."

"Which I would have immediately pushed her from when I realized she was not Lady Borthwick."

Her head lifted, her vision blurring as she looked back at him. "I believe you." It was the second time she had said such a thing, the second time she saw the very same reaction to his expression, except this time, he smiled.

"I do not take your belief for granted, Miss Ainsley." Lifting his hand, he let his thumb brush away her tears, skimming across her skin. "I am sorry."

"I do not know what we are to do., Lord Northwick. I did not ever expect this of my sister. I am horrified if —"

"Which is why we must wait and see." Lord Northwick spoke calmly, his words quietening her fractious thoughts. "Forgive me, I do not mean to speak over you, but neither do

I want you to become overly concerned. We have no assurance it *is* Miss Bettina Ainsley. Yes, her letter looked similar to the first note and as for the library, I..."

Jane's heart ached with both gratitude and sorrow as Lord Northwick attempted to come up with an explanation as to how she could have known about the library before Jane had even mentioned it. He was doing his utmost to calm her and how much she appreciated his consideration.

"Mayhap you *did* mention the library before even being aware of it. That is a possibility, surely?"

Jane's eyes began to drown with fresh tears, not only with concern for her sister but also at the kindness in Lord Northwick's face. He was being so very sympathetic, attempting to understand her distress and doing what he could to aid her. His words were meant to soften the pain he knew, no doubt, that would soon be coming. Her heart yearned for him and without being aware of it, she moved forward. Before she knew what she was doing, her head was on his shoulder, her hands free from his, and now pressed up against his chest. Lord Northwick let out some sort of soft exclamation but the very next moment, his hands went around her waist and he held her tightly. It was just as well they could not be seen either by their companions or by those at the window for Jane was sure something would have been said, some consequences would follow and yet, despite such concerns, she could not help herself. It had been more than just a want, it had been a need. A need to be close to him, a need to breathe him in, to let the assurance he brought settle in her heart.

"Miss Ainsley."

Something strangled through Lord Northwick's voice and when she lifted her head, a jolt ran straight through her also, stealing away her voice and leaving her staring up into his face, mute. In an instant, she forgot all about her sister, forgot about the notes and the difficulties that surrounded her and instead found herself looking at his face, wondering why her heart was beating so tumultuously.

"Miss Ainsley."

This time, Lord Northwick's voice was so low, it was only above a whisper.

"We must..."

His eyes squeezed closed, his jaw tightened as his hands fell from her waist, as though it had taken him a great effort to do so. He could not move back, for the tree was behind him and thus Jane was forced to move away from him.

Embarrassment flooded her and she dropped her head. "Forgive me, Lord Northwick." She could give no explanation, no reason as to what she had done or why, still utterly confused at why she had practically thrown herself into his arms.

"There is no need to apologize." Lord Northwick cleared his throat brusquely, twisting his head away. "It is only that we ought not to be too far away from the other guests."

"Of course." The flush burning her cheeks seemed to wind its way through her entire frame as she stepped back even further, keeping her head low. "Forgive me. It was I who stood too close."

A gentle hand lifted her chin, his touch sending a shiver through her as she unwillingly looked up into Lord Northwick's face. His eyes seemed lighter than ever before, swirling with hints of green and gold, focused and intent. "I am so very glad you did, Miss Ainsley."

The warmth of his smile settled her embarrassment a little. She was uncomfortable, even mortified over her own unguarded behavior, and yet she did not feel even a single ounce of regret. It was as if her heart was glad over what she had done, unwilling to hold even a flicker of regret. It had been bold, of course, far too bold for someone such as her yet, in this moment, gazing into Lord Northwick's face, Jane was glad she had chosen to draw near.

"I should tell you that I have received another note." Offering her his arm, they quickly fell into step together, coming back into the view of the other guests, who were now some distance away. Jane's heart quickened a little, but it was not for fear of being discovered so far from them, but rather over what Lord Northwick was now telling her.

"Bettina has written to you again." Even saying her sister's name in such a context made her shudder, with Lord Northwick immediately reaching across to press her hand.

"Yes, she has." His voice was grave, sighing heavily as he shook his head. "She begs me to come to the arbor this evening at a particular hour, *if*, of course, I am interested in warming myself with her embraces – which I am not, you understand." His hand squeezed her fingers and then fell back to his side. "I could easily simply refuse to appear. My absence would bring the matter to an end, would it not?"

"It may," Jane agreed, her stomach beginning to swirl uncomfortably. "Or it may encourage her. If you do not appear, perhaps she will think she must offer herself to you a little more... visibly. No, Lord Northwick, you should go. And I shall go with you."

A long breath exhaled from him. "If you are sure, it would be a good idea." Sharp eyes dotted to hers. "If the two of us are discovered in an arbor in the middle of the evening, then I can only imagine what would be – "

"Then let us ask Lord Renforth to join us again, since he already knows the circumstances. His presence would keep us quite safe, would it not? I am certain no one will miss me from the evening, however. There will be so much going on that everyone will be far too entertained to notice. I am sure that is why my sister has made such an arrangement." Her stomach knotted and she winced visibly. "At some point this evening, I shall lose her. She will step away and no doubt, I will find myself distracted enough so as not to realize until it is much too late."

"I hope it will not be as you say." Lord Northwick murmured. "I suppose, if it is your sister waiting there, you intend to take a course of action thereafter to prevent her from ruining herself entirely by behaving in the same way with another gentleman?"

Jane swallowed but nodded. "It is my intention." Taking in a great breath. Jane allowed her eyes to close for a moment. "I am afraid, if it is to be as we both believe, I shall have to speak to my mother about what I have discovered." The thought sent a coldness sweeping through her for, after all, she knew precisely what such a thing could mean for Bettina. But it could not be helped, she reminded herself. To have her sister behave in such a way as this might not bring only Bettina's name into disfavor, but Jane's also. It could tie scandal to their family name, could bind them *all* in the shadow of it for many years to come. It simply had to be prevented.

As if he had known what she was thinking, Lord Northwick squeezed her arm very gently indeed. "You do know *I* should never turn my back on you, regardless of what happens," he told her softly. "I would never have taken your sister into my arms and never shall, regardless of what her desire might be. I want to assure you of my own determination."

Jane looked to him, seeing the gentleness in his eyes, the slightly pinched expression that spoke of concern and found such an affection building in her heart she fought to hide it from him. "I am humble enough to admit I misjudged you." Licking her lips briefly, she offered him a smile. "You have been nothing but kind to me, showing both consideration and concern. I am aware there may be hints of the rogue about you but, as you have said, all gentlemen, on the whole, can be that way and I should not have judged you so harshly."

"But there shall be no more hints of such a thing, I promise you." Lord Northwick did not take his eyes from hers, his steps slowing. "I beg of you to believe me when I say I have no desire to be anything but a stalwart gentleman from this day forward. You have built something within me, something I cannot quite comprehend, but it is something that urges me forward towards being the very best of gentlemen." One shoulder lifted. "Mayhap you will think me foolish, but I –"

"No, never."

Jane spoke quickly, her hand slipping a little from his arm as she turned to face him. "No, indeed, I do not find anything you say foolish. I find your words to be... full of sweetness, Lord Northwick." Her heart quickened, but she continued on, a driving need to tell him all growing steadily. "You express the most wonderful things and I think–"

"And what is it the King and Queen are concocting now? You have one more task to set the guests before this evening!"

The loud exclamation of Lady Meyrick cut Jane's conversation sharply, and she forced her attention back to the lady, seeing how many of the others were now also turned to face them.

"I should inform you, Your Majesties, I have a grand evening's entertainment planned, in honor of you both –

our Christmas King and Queen!" Laughing, she turned sparkling eyes to the rest of the guests. "It shall be very enjoyable for us all!"

"We are both very much looking forward to it, Lady Meyrick."

Lord Northwick's answer seemed to please Lady Meyrick for she turned and began to walk again, leaving Lord Northwick to rub one hand over his chin, his lips pulling to one side.

"It seems as though in the midst of all of this, you and I must also come up with some confounded task for our guests."

Smiling, she took his arm again. "I am certain we can come up with something. After all, we seem to have done very well together thus far, have we not?"

Lord Northwick gave her one long look, and it took a moment before his smile appeared. "Yes." Murmuring softly, he moved a little closer as they began to walk together. "Yes, I believe I would agree with you, Miss Ainsley. We do very well together indeed."

CHAPTER THIRTEEN

"Are you quite prepared?"

Lucius grimaced as Lord Renforth came to stand beside him.

"It is almost time."

"Yes, I am aware." Sighing, he shook his head. "This is not the most pleasant of experiences, I shall admit."

Lord Renforth nodded, looking out at the grounds as they stood just inside the front door of the manor house. There had been a light snowfall, and with the fires that now burned merrily in the gardens, everything seemed to either glow or sparkle. There were so many entertainments, Lucius did not think he would be able to see all of them before the evening was out and thus far, no one had come back shivering into the house, complaining of the cold.

He took a breath, aware of just how heavy his spirits were as he rubbed one hand over his eyes. "We must find Miss Ainsley."

"There is no need. I am here."

The gentle voice of Miss Ainsley called Lucius's attention, and he turned sharply, seeing her walking into the house towards them. Her cheeks were flushed, but her green eyes sparkled gently, although her lips pulled from a smile into a tight line. He could not imagine what she must be feeling at this present moment, quite certain that fear for her sister was the driving need within her. How much he wished to comfort her! How much he wished to take this burden from her shoulders, and yet the only way to do so would be to confront her sister.

"Good evening, Miss Ainsley." Lucius took a breath, his gaze flickering down her as his heart responded to her presence with a sudden cavorting. She was dressed in a dark green gown with a thick cloak over the top. To Lucius' eyes, she looked like the most magnificent creature he had ever seen. Why had he ever so much as glanced at another lady? There was none as beautiful as Miss Ainsley. The desire to be beside her grew sharply, forcing his feet forward.

"How are you, my dear lady?" Making his way across towards her, he took both of her hands, fully aware they were in full view of many of the other guests, but finding he cared very little.

"I am well, all things considered." Biting the edge of her lip, Miss Ainsley took in a deep breath. "It is almost over, is it not?"

Lucius, look down into her face, resisting the urge to place one hand to her cheek. He wished very much this heaviness was gone from her already, that the whole situation was at an end. "You need not come with me, Miss Ainsley. I will have Lord Renforth with me, as you suggested. He will be able to make it quite plain to Bett – to whoever it is sitting within the arbor –I have no desire to take them into my arms."

For there is only one person I wish to be there.

He did not speak this a final sentence aloud, but

somehow he believed she knew what he was thinking. A soft smile touched the edge of her lips, and for a moment, they simply gazed back at one another.

"Alas, I think I must." With a small sigh, Miss Ainsley dropped her gaze, turning her head away a little. "I want my sister to know I have learned what she is doing. I want her to see it cannot continue."

The weight of responsibility settled in Lucius' chest. "Very well." Stepping to one side, he offered her his arm. "Then let us go."

The three of them stepped into the dark together, making their way around the many guests. The fire-breathers and the jugglers were entertaining a good many of the guests and none so much as glanced at them. Lucius had already made his way here once before, knowing precisely where he was to go, and thus it did not take him long to reach the path that led to the arbor. The gardens were still lit by torches in various places, and Lucius was grateful for them, for while they did not take away any of the chill, they lit his path. Their feet crunched on the gravel until, after some minutes of walking in silence, they came near to the arbor.

"Hold." Miss Ainsley came to a stop, her hand now clutching his arm. "You should go first, Lord Northwick."

A little confused, Lucius turned to face her. "I do not understand why."

"Because," she began, dropping her head a little in obvious embarrassment. "If by some luck, it is *not* my sister, if there is some small chance it is someone else, then I would rather you came upon them alone rather than the three of us trampling upon their presence. Our arrival would bring a great shame to them, would it not?"

Drawing in a deep breath, Lucius found her hand in the

darkness and let his fingers twine through hers. "I assure you, I have no intention of permitting any young woman – any lady at all, in fact, to grasp my attention."

"I am well aware and I believe you," came the reply, those words bringing a gentle smile to his face. This was the third time he had heard her speak them, and as yet they had not stopped bringing joy to his heart. "Lord Renforth and I will walk a little behind you. If it is my sister, then I will hear her voice soon enough, and if it is not, then he can take me back to the party."

Lucius glanced towards his friend, who nodded, the firelight flickering yellow and gold across each of their faces.

"Very well." There was a strange tightness in his chest that he could not seem to chase away, no matter how deeply he breathed. This was awkwardness itself, desperation growing in his heart as he held Miss Ainsley's gaze, praying silently it was anyone other than Miss Bettina Ainsley waiting for him there, simply so there might be less pain for Miss Jane. "Stay nearby."

The steadiness of her gaze spoke of the trust she had in him and it was with that trust in his heart, Lucius then stepped away.

His feet crunched lightly, but he walked with great purpose, making his way to the arbor without any hesitation. It was darker here now, and Lucius took a few moments to allow his eyes to adjust. Taking a deep breath, he cleared his throat, then with one hand on the edge of the arbor, he came around inside it. There was something of a door and a small roof over the top but it did not keep out much of the wind, nor the chill – but it hid the lady waiting for him very well indeed. There was a rustle of skirts, and Lucius quickly drew back, not wishing to step into the arbor any deeper.

"I have come as you have asked." His voice was low, his jaw fixing tight. "Reveal yourself to me."

"I should be very glad to do so." The giggling, high-pitched voice was one he immediately recognized, and his stomach dropped to the ground. It seemed both he and Miss Ainsley had been correct. The person in the arbor, waiting for him, the person who had sent those notes, was none other than Miss Bettina Ainsley.

"I was so disappointed our meeting at the library was interrupted." The young woman came closer, her outline barely visible. "But now you have come, now you are here! You could not stay away from me."

"I am come here, but not for the reasons you think." Lucius spoke starkly, holding nothing back. "Understand this: I have no desire to be at all close to you. You are being foolish in behaving this way."

The young woman laughed, her hand suddenly touching his arm, forcing Lucius to jerk back.

"Why, you are a little jittery, are you not?" Her hand came again, grasping his wrist and holding on with such a tightness, Lucius could not shake her off for fear of injuring her in the darkness. "Have you not also been pursuing me? Surely you must have known it was *I* who wrote those notes during this house party?"

Lucius cleared his throat. This was not the way he wanted the conversation to go. "Miss Ainsley, you must not –"

"Did you not see the eagerness in my eyes the night of the masquerade ball? Did you not see how willing I was to go with you?" She moved a little nearer. "I saw you that night. I saw you with your mask, so clear and obvious in the manner of it. You wanted to be seen, wanted me – and the other ladies – to know who you were. Of course, I came to speak to you! How could I not when you appeared to be so... obvious? I could not help but whisper encouragements and I am sure I saw you smile when I spoke them to you."

Her voice dropped a little to a slightly coy tone and Lucius shuddered, taking a step back and trying to pull his arm away, only for Miss Bettina to go with him.

"I did not think it was you who spoke to me that night, no." Speaking with as much fierceness as he could muster and clearly as he could, so Miss Jane Ainsley and Lord Renforth could hear him, Lucius attempted to detach himself from the young woman. "I thought you were Lady Borthwick. *She* was the one I was seeking out and it was only quite by accident I took your hand instead of hers. Your gowns were very similar and therefore, it was a complete mistake. You must believe that!"

"Now you are teasing me." She laughed again, but the sound only pushed Lucius further away. "Those words were the excuse you gave my sister, but I certainly do not believe it."

"In that regard, I can assure you that *you* are the one mistaken." Lucius lifted his chin, taking another step out of the arbor, so the flame light might illuminate the situation a little more. "I am not a scoundrel. I may have been roguish in my behavior at times, but I am certainly *not* a gentleman who would ever take advantage of a young lady such as yourself. You are mistaken," he said again, more vehemently this time. "I did not come here to find you so I might accept your warm embraces."

"Why then did you come?" The lady's voice was light and teasing, and it was only when her sister's voice broke through the air that her hand finally fell away from Lucius' arm.

"He came so I might see you, so I could confirm my

suspicions, and so I could drag you away from this foolish path before you make the most monumental mistake."

There was a breath of silence.

"J – Jane?" The confidence that had been in Bettina's voice was gone, fading away, leaving only a small and broken whisper. "Whatever are you doing here?"

"It is as I have said." The confidence in Miss Jane's voice grew ever stronger as she came to stand directly next to Lucius, her hand finding his in the darkness. Her fingers curled around his, clinging on fiercely, as though he was the only one giving her the strength to stand upright.

"I cannot believe you are the one who has done this, Bettina. I can hardly take it in."

"I- I did not think ...."

"You did not think I would ever discover it was you." Miss Jane continued to speak with a clear decisiveness as Lucius drew in a deep breath, finding himself both comforted and relieved the matter was now at its end. "I was wrong about Lord Northwick, he is *not* a scoundrel. He is not a self- ish, arrogant gentleman but rather someone who has kindness and concern – concern for you also, I might add. When he began to suspect you were the one writing him these notes, he was desperate not to inform me so I would not be troubled. However, on the night I informed you about the note in his pocket after the Christmas ball, you mentioned the library when I myself had never given such information to you."

There was a moment's pause and when she took in another breath, Lucius caught how it shook. "You have given yourself away," she continued, a little more quietly now. "And now it is for me to make certain you are never able to behave in such a manner again."

"But you do not understand!" Miss Bettina Ainsley

began to wail, sounding more like a petulant child than a young, educated woman. "I have seen my friends flirt and tease and enjoy all manner of attentions from various gentlemen of the *ton*, but I am told to refrain from such things! They tease me for being so foolish and prim, and what they spoke of sounds so very exciting, I simply *had* to experience it for myself! Why should I not enjoy myself when I am given opportunity?"

"Because you give no thought to the consequences that would follow thereafter." Lucius found himself speaking in response, his voice low. "Had I been a scoundrel, Miss Ainsley, then I certainly would have taken advantage of you. What would have happened, then? What if we had been discovered? You might well have been ruined and your reputation sullied, as well as the name of your family. For a single foolish moment, you would have given away your entire future. Is such foolhardiness truly something you wish to pursue?"

Miss Jane did not give her sister a chance to answer, speaking so quickly after him, there was barely a breath between them. "I do not think I have ever been more ashamed of you. Come with me at once. We are going to find Mother."

The gasp from Miss Bettina's throat was not unexpected, and her petulant cries for forgiveness rang in the air around them.

Lucius pressed Miss Jane's fingers and then released her hand, allowing the lady to step to one side, gesturing for her sister to make her way along the path. After a few moments, and with the stamping of one foot on the ground, the young woman went.

Miss Jane Ainsley let out a slow breath, pressed one

hand to her heart as Lord Renforth quickly stepped after the first Miss Ainsley.

"My dear Jane."

Lucius spoke softly so only she could hear, reaching out one hand to her – only for the lady to fling herself into his arms. He could do nothing other than hold her as arms went about her waist, feeling her sob into his shoulder. He wanted to say something to comfort her, wanted to do something more that would dry her tears, but there was nothing to be done. Instead, he simply held her close, waiting for the pain to subside a little and, after a few moments she recovered herself enough to lift her head.

"I am so very grateful to you, Northwick." Her voice was broken with tears and Lucius lifted one hand, brushing moisture from her cheeks as it glistened in the moonlight. "It is at an end, but I cannot tell you how brokenhearted I am to realize it was my sister, after all."

"She is young," Lucius remarked quietly, "and perhaps a little foolish. I am sure that, come the summertime, she will be a much changed young lady."

"If she is given another summer Season," came the sad reply. "It may be my father will decide to find her a husband of his own choosing rather than allow her a preference."

Lucius nodded sagely. "It may turn out to be the best thing for her." He let his hand linger at her cheek for a moment before dropping his hand, sensing her moving back before she even took a step.

"I will come and find you again very soon." Her hand slowly released his, as though she were reluctant to move away. "I cannot thank you enough for all you have done and the consideration you have shown to us both. It is greatly appreciated."

"I have come to care for you so very deeply, Miss Ainsley." Before he could prevent it, the words were tumbling from him. "I want only to see you smile, to see you happy. It may be this difficult time will lead to that, for sometimes difficulties must be faced before true happiness can be found."

She smiled at him then, tears still shining in her eyes. "Let us hope it does, Lord Northwick, for I am quite ready for a little happiness." Without another word, she turned on her heel and followed after her sister.

CHAPTER FOURTEEN

"Jane, please do not go to Mama!"

Jane pressed her lips together hard, trying to calm her whirling nerves. It was now the following morning, for Jane had not been able to speak with her mother the previous evening. When they had found Lady Wilkinson, she had been a little too merry for calm conversation so thus, instead, Jane had instructed her sister to take herself to her bedchamber while she considered what she would do thereafter.

It had been a difficult evening and Jane had found herself following after her sister soon afterwards, a little afraid Bettina had not gone back to her room as she had been asked. The moment she had stepped inside, however, Bettina had launched herself at her, seemingly distraught over the entire situation. Having managed to get a little sleep, Jane was now, at present, intending to go and speak with her mother about everything she had learned, despite Bettina's cries to the contrary.

"I swear I shall never do such a thing again." Bettina came to stand in front of the door, blocking Jane's access. "If you speak to Mama, I will be left without any choice as to my future. You know such a thing will occur, do you not? I will be given to some gentleman of Father's choosing. I will be forced to marry and will have no opportunity to return to London."

Jane drew in a deep breath, battling against the sympathy in her chest. "What if such a situation is in your best interest?" she said softly, seeing the way her sister's eyes flared. "Surely you must understand the severity of what you have done, Bettina. You cannot imagine my shock on realizing it was you who had been sending those notes to Lord Northwick – notes you began when we were back in London during the summer Season."

"And I have explained to you why I wanted to do so."

"All the same, it concerns me." Jane took one of her sister's hands, but Bettina pulled it away. "I do not mean to speak harshly, but you have been remarkably foolish. I can have no assurance you will not do the same again."

"Not even if I swear it to you?"

Jane shook her head. "I doubt such a thing would make any difference. You could easily begin writing notes to another gentleman without anyone's knowledge – a gentleman who could be a good deal less honorable than Lord Northwick, I might add."

Bettina shook her head. "I am sure you are mistaken to think of all gentlemen in such a way, just as you were wrong to consider Lord Northwick in that same ill fashion." Her arms folded across her chest. "Gentlemen only offer embraces and kisses. I may be young but I have never experienced a gentleman taking me into his arms. Why should I wait until I am wed for such a thing to take place?"

The foolishness of her sister hit Jane hard and she dropped her head forward, one hand passing over her eyes.

"My dear Bettina, you cannot truly be this naïve." Her sister frowned, a ripple of doubt in her features as Jane's heart grew even heavier. "Yes, some gentlemen will behave so, but some will not. They may take you in their arms and offer you a few gentle kisses, Bettina but then seek to push you further. Imagine what would occur if you were caught in that sort of predicament! Not every gentleman will be careful about whether or not they can be seen, for some will simply step away and care very little as to whether or not their reputation is soiled. Some delight in being called a rogue but you, however, will be given no escape. A few stolen moments could bring ruin to yourself and shame to your family."

Bettina swallowed hard, her face suddenly pale and Jane breathed out slowly, seeing Bettina now appearing to be taking in the matter with a good deal more seriousness.

"I do not...." Bettina passed one hand over her eyes. "My friends, they never once said such a thing. I was only eager for..." She trailed off for the second time, squeezing her eyes closed as a single tear dropped to her cheek. "I thought Lord Northwick was a rogue and, during the summer Season, he was also the only gentlemen none of my friends were considering. I confess I saw your closeness with him and found myself ashamed of my own behavior, although I did not stop it." She lifted her head and Jane closed her eyes, somewhere between sadness and relief. "I want to assure you I have never had any feelings for Lord Northwick – nothing genuine at all. In my own mind, I believed you would never really draw close to Lord North-wick, not after what you said about him from the beginning, and yet when I became aware of your interest in him, I should have stepped back." Her tear-stained face lifted to

Jane's. "But I did not. I can see now I have been selfish and foolish."

Jane's heart twisted and she took in a long breath, her shoulders lifting. "I am relieved you can see that, Bettina. And yes, I will admit to you now I find my heart is somewhat involved with the gentleman."

Bettina took Jane's hand, her gaze suddenly steadying. "If you speak to Mother, she will wish to remove me from this house at once." Her hand tightened gently. "That might mean you and Lord Northwick will not be able to bring to any sort of conclusion what is currently growing between you."

Sighing, Jane shook her head. "Regardless, I must think of you and you only. All the same...." Biting her lip hard, she looked into her sister's face, seeing the change in her expression and finding herself somewhat convinced Bettina was taking this all with a great deal of seriousness. "I will consider the matter a little longer. If there is even the smallest hint of misbehavior from you within the next few days, however, then be assured I will go directly to our mother. I say such things, not as a threat, but because I am concerned for you." Her heart constricted as Bettina's hand fell away. "You may not like this Bettina, but it is for the best."

Her sister shoulders rounded as she dropped her head. "I understand. Truly, I do."

This was the first time Jane's heart believed Bettina had truly grasped the seriousness of what she had done. On instinct, she reached out to hug her sister and Bettina immediately leaned into the embrace, beginning to sob, her shoulders shaking. Jane closed her eyes, her own tears not far away.

"Come." Pulling back, she tugged out her handkerchief

and handed it to Bettina who quickly dabbed at her eyes. "Let us go. We are to have an excellent day, I am sure. Now we have all broken our fast, Lady Meyrick will surely have some sort of game waiting in the drawing room."

"I do not feel I can take part in such a thing."

A wry laugh escaped from Jane's lips. "I have felt that way many a time this Season, but we shall bring ourselves to do it this morning also. Mayhap we will find some enjoyment in it after a while."

"Perhaps." Bettina looked up at her again, taking Jane's again for a moment. "I want you to know I appreciate your consideration." She swallowed, pressing the handkerchief to her eyes again. "It seems I have been more foolish than I realized."

"You have, but let us both put it from our mind for the present." Squeezing her sister's hand, she managed a smile. "We need to go and join the others. We can talk about this matter again later, if it requires it."

"Thank you, Jane."

"There you are."

It was now after luncheon and, as yet, Jane had not had a moment's opportunity to speak to Lord Northwick, for Lady Meyrick and the Duke himself had kept their guests busy before luncheon. The fact she had been sitting across the table from Lord Northwick had meant they could not have even a word or two of conversation and it was only now they seemed able to speak freely. The second she had stepped inside, Lord Northwick was on his feet, coming across towards her.

"How do you fare, Miss Ainsley? I have been so very eager to speak with you, but have been prevented thus far."

His voice was low as he reached to touch her fingers with his for the briefest moment. Amidst the hubbub of noise from the other guests who were all talking and laughing amongst each other, his direct attention towards Jane was not noticed by many, although Jane herself felt overwhelming gratitude at his consideration. Surreptitiously, she grasped his hand for a moment, her body warming all the more at their brief connection.

"I am well." Smiling at how the light returned to his eyes, pulling away the frown had been on his forehead as he had waited to hear what she was going to say. "I have spoken to my sister at length both last night and this morning. I believe she is beginning to realize the seriousness of what she has done."

"I am very glad to hear it." He smiled, then gestured to the other side of the room. "Might you wish for some tea? There has been some laid out over here."

Hesitating, Jane curled her fingers over his. "Actually, Lord Northwick, what I wish for the most is to have a few minutes to speak with you in private." After what she had shared with her sister, Jane now had an urge to express the very same to Lord Northwick himself. She did not know where such feelings had come from, but one way or another, they needed to be expressed. It would do her no good to keep them hidden; she had to let him know just how grateful she was for all he had done in protecting her sister *and* in protecting her. If he had chosen to do the precise opposite, had chosen to take advantage of what Bettina had offered him, then the situation might now be very different indeed, but he had not done so. He had refrained and stepped back. He had protected. He had shielded them both and there she could not think of doing anything other than making him aware of her sincere thanks.

Alas, it was much too late, for Lady Meyrick quickly garnered everyone's attention in her usual way and Jane's request to speak with Lord Northwick privately was gone. With a frustrated sigh, she directed her attention towards the lady in question, having no choice but to do as was expected.

"As you all know, the young ladies of this house have been very hard working indeed, creating beautiful Christmas decorations for the Duke's house." Her eyes glittered. "However, I have hidden some sprigs of mistletoe in amongst the decorations and require them to be found! There are fifteen to be discovered. Are you all quite ready?"

There was no choice given as to whether or not Jane wished to take part, but she suddenly found herself very eager indeed to join in, which was most unlike her. The thought of finding a mistletoe with Lord Northwick sent such a flurry of excitement through her that Jane caught her breath, one hand pressing lightly against it. When Lord Northwick lifted an eyebrow questioningly, she merely shook her head, too embarrassed at her own reaction and her own thoughts to say anything by way of explanation.

"Miss Ainsley, if you should like to go with me on this search, we will be able to talk then?" the gentleman suggested and without a breath of hesitation, Jane took his proffered arm before, together, they walked from the room. They were the last ones to exit the drawing room for almost everyone else of the unmarried young ladies and gentlemen scurried away, with someone scampering away so quickly, she pushed hard against Jane as she did so, making her stumble. Lord Northwick caught and steadied her quickly, and Jane threw him a grateful smile, a little overwhelmed.

"I fear this task is already bringing out the worst in some of us." Lord Northwick chuckled and Jane could not help but smile, aware of the quickening of her heart as they came to the long hallway where no-one else was present. Anticipation ran over her skin, sending gooseflesh over her arms as she continued to walk alongside him. "While I have an opportunity, Lord Northwick, I do wish to tell you how grateful I am to you."

"Grateful?" he repeated, appearing rather surprised. "I do not think there is much you need to thank me for."

She smiled at him. "I would disagree in the strongest terms, Lord Northwick. You have been *more* than considerate when it comes to my sister."

Lord Northwick shook his hand. "Again, you think too highly of me. It is not as though I was about to tell everyone present what your sister had been doing."

"Some gentlemen may have done so." Jane held his gaze for a moment, their steps slowing even more. "And worse, some might have been eager to take her offer for themselves, as I am sure you well know."

His shoulders dropped. "That is true, although I would not have done so."

Jane smiled back at him. "I believe everything you have said." Moving a little closer to him, she moved her free hand to his arm, as though she might be able to convey her fervency through a single touch. "My regard for you, my respect for your character, and my regret over my previous harsh judgement must be known to you by now. I feel these things deeply. I wish you very much to know how appreciative I am of your solidarity with me. Your openness and your honesty, as well as your delicacy over matters with Bettina, has pulled every ounce of worry from my heart. I believe your word can be trusted."

His features softened. "You are very kind, Miss Ainsley, although I must also confess my foolishness. On the night of the masquerade ball, I ought to have ignored the note pressed into my pocket. I should have stayed far from such a thing, for would that not have been a behavior of a gentleman?" Shaking his head, he took in a breath, his lips twisting. "I see it now. I did not behave as I ought to have done."

Her hands slipped from his arm and ran down to join with his fingers instead.

"I understand that to have a closer connection with one specific lady is far better than a brief moment stolen here or there." Lord Northwick's dark eyes lingered on hers, and something exploded within Jane's heart. There was no guile here; not a word of a lie was being spoken. Everything Lord Northwick was telling her was the truth, coming straight from his heart – and she was filled with joy in hearing it.

"I should like...." The truth she wanted to then present to him by way of exchange seemed to stick to her lips, her heart pounding as she gazed into his eyes. "I should like to express to you that my consideration of you has now grown into..." Swallowing, she closed her eyes briefly. "Into a gentle affection for you. It is something I never expected but I now believe, the longer I spend with you, the more I shall feel it."

"And is that truly a great fear of yours?" Lord Northwick smiled a little sadly as she looked back at him. "For if it is, then I confess I shall be gravely disappointed."

"Indeed it is not!" An urgency to explain herself had her stepping closer to him, her hands rested on his forearms as if she wanted to pull herself near. "There is no fear in my heart over what I feel, Lord Northwick. Rather, I find myself so utterly captivated by it."

Her answer made his eyes dance. "I am very pleased to hear you speak so honestly and to know there is no fear nor regret in your heart, Miss Ainsley, is a joy. Your words give me the courage to tell you the truth. I confess I have been a little hesitant in sharing my own truth with you, given the strange difficulties you and I have faced these last few weeks."

A sudden thought constricted Jane's heart as she pressed one hand to it. "Share it with me, Lord Northwick. I beg of you to share it with me without delay." There was a slight huskiness to her voice, a rasping that spoke of her swirling emotions. "Do not make me wait even a little longer."

"Ah, there you both are."

The anticipation that had built like a wall in Jane's heart was quickly knocked asunder as her sister suddenly came around the corner of the hallway, accompanied by their mother. The lady in question appeared rather confused as to why Bettina had taken her through the Duke's house in search of Jane, frowning heavily as she drew near. Jane instinctively took a step back from Lord Northwick, for the last thing she required was for her mother to berate her for walking alone with a gentleman, despite the fact they were playing a game set by Lady Meyrick.

"*Now,* will you tell the meaning of this, Bettina?" Lady Wilkinson asked, her gaze switching from one daughter to the next. "I was quite ready to take tea with Lady Meyrick as she waited for you all to return, only for you to drag me away! I believe we have been wandering around this place for at least half an hour!"

Jane knew all too well it certainly could not be half an hour, given she had been walking with Lord Northwick for only a few minutes. Putting this down to her mother's irritations at being so pulled away, relief flooded her chest as her mother said nothing about Lord Northwick's presence. It seemed that in games such as these, propriety was not as much of a concern as it usually was.

Bettina lifted her chin a little. "I brought you here so we might speak to Jane, Mama."

Jane's gaze lurched to her sister. Whatever was it Bettina was going to do? Could it be that her sister was about to state something about Jane's affection for Lord Northwick to their mother? And if she was, whatever would have driven her to such a thing?

"I hope I will not embarrass either you or Lord Northwick, Jane," Bettina continued after a moment's pause. "But I must be truthful."

"Truthful about what, my dear girl?" Lady Wilkinson set her jaw, her gaze a little narrowed.

Bettina took in a long, slow breath. "I must tell you, Mama, I have spoken to Jane, and I had begged her to keep this to herself. Whether it was right of me or not I cannot say, but in the last few hours, I have had a long time to consider what Jane said to me. Finding myself back in the company of the other esteemed guests, I have realized my behavior cannot continue. It must, therefore, be made known."

Jane swallowed against the growing ache in her throat. She had not expected this from Bettina, but it was obvious now her younger sister had decided to speak openly to her mother. Lady Wilkinson's eyes went from Bettina to Lord Northwick, the lines on her forehead increasing with an obvious confusion to what her younger daughter was going to say.

"I was wrong to ask you to keep it to yourself, Jane." Bettina's gaze was bold, her words determined. "After our conversation, I have had a chance to consider and now have had a change of heart. Hearing the warnings you gave me, I reflected upon my actions."

"Bettina." Jane put a comforting hand on her sister's arm. "I hope I was not too harsh in my words."

Bettina smiled ruefully and shook her head. "No, you were not. You made me rather terrified about what consequences could have followed had I continued on as I intended."

Lady Wilkinson let out a long, frustrated sigh, throwing up one hand. "In heaven's name, will someone *please* tell me what is going on!"

Jane glanced to Lord Northwick, aware of the frown lines on his forehead. Would he prefer not to be present while they spoke of this? Or would he be glad the truth was finally out? Her sister must have had the very same thought, for Bettina immediately inquired as to whether Lord Northwick would be contented for her to speak openly. With a brief nod, he directed her attention again to Lady Wilkinson and, to Jane's delight, reached out so she might take his arm. She took it eagerly, all too aware of how her mother's eyes glanced at this, leading to a slight lift of her eyebrows, but was relieved when nothing was said.

"Mother, I have been foolish."

With a great breath, Bettina turned to face Lady Wilkinson. "I have been writing notes to particular gentlemen. I have been doing so anonymously in the hope one of them will respond to me."

Jane's breath curled in her chest, her eyes suddenly going very wide indeed. "Bettina." Her hoarse voice was barely audible, even to her own ears. "Do you mean to say Lord Northwick was not the only gentleman you wrote to?

Swallowing hard, her sister nodded, her eyes bright with tears. "Yes. That is so. There is so much shame in admitting this." She put one hand to her heart, her head dropping. "But I know I must."

Jane closed her eyes, aware of the tears burning and the dull throbbing in her heart.

"I grew tired of always being so very proper, Mama. I grew jealous of my friends telling me of the gentlemen that swept them up into their arms. I believe even Miss Bridget was kissed by one specific gentleman! And then some of them laughed at me for having never experienced the same as they."

Jane's heart softened with sympathy, for while her sister had been foolish, could she not understand her behavior in light of such treatment from Bettina's so-called friends?

"If I might?" Lord Northwick tilted his head just a little. "Did it ever occur to you, Miss Ainsley, that your friends might not have been telling you the truth?

Bettina blinked, the color draining from her face.

"You are aware, I am sure, young ladies often tell stories," Lord Northwick continued, speaking a little more softly now. "Could it be that some – not all – of your friends made-up such stories, simply in order to appear as you your-self wish to be?"

Bettina dropped her head, her eyes squeezing closed as a single tear fell to her cheek. "I... I could not say for certain but perhaps you are right. I did not even think about such a possibility." There was tightness to her voice that had not been there before as her naivete became all the clearer. Jane pressed her lips tight together as she looked to her mother, seeing Lady Wilkinson pass one hand over her forehead.

"Bettina." Lady Wilkinson did not appear in any way angry. Rather her gaze was soft as she came closer to her younger daughter. "You say you were attempting to elicit the attentions of a gentleman - any gentleman - rather than behave in the proper manner, as you have been guided?"

Bettina opened her eyes, lifted her head, and then nodded, her lips trembling. Jane did not know what to say, for to hear her sister admitting such a thing was painful indeed. There was reason behind what she had done, yes, but the fact she had written to more than one gentleman made Jane's heart twist with an agonized fear of what could have taken place had one of them taken Bettina's offer to their heart.

"You are very lucky indeed. No gentleman sought to take advantage of your proposals," she found herself murmuring as both her mother and Lord Northwick nodded in agreement. "But surely, Mama, Bettina's honesty in this is admirable. She has done nothing to endanger her name as yet."

"Unless you intend to put your name to yet more notes?" The warning in their mother's voice was significant, but as Bettina lifted her head, yet more fear clutched at Jane's heart. After a moment, however, Bettina shook her head and relief flooded back into Jane, letting out a slow breath as she clutched Lord Northwick's arm a little more tightly.

Lady Wilkinson closed her eyes briefly, then opened them. "Then all is well." Wrapping one arm around Bettina's shoulders, she took another moment before she spoke again. "This behavior is to stop at once, however."

Bettina hung her head. "I am well aware I must do so, Mama. "Putting out one hand towards Jane, Bettina managed a small smile, despite the tears in her eyes. "Had it not been for Jane, I do not think I would have realized the seriousness of my actions."

"It is as well you have such a considerate sister."

Much to Jane's surprise, her mother moved forward to embrace her, and Lord Northwick took a small step back. Her mother pressed both hands to Jane's face, looking at her for a long moment, before smiling and wrapping her arms around her.

"You have always taken such a great responsibility for your sister." Moving back to Bettina, she wrapped one arm around Bettina's shoulders again. "It is good you chose to be honest also, Bettina. I am grateful to you both."

"I do hope you can forgive my foolishness also, Lord Northwick." Bettina could not seem to lift her eyes to his, her head and gaze still low, but Lord Northwick responded immediately.

"There is no harm done, Miss Ainsley." His soft voice was a balm to Jane's grieved spirits. "I am glad you have been able to be honest with your mother. Please know all I did in this matter was to make certain you were not injured in any way. I do want the best for you."

"You are very kind," came the reply, as her mother murmured the very same compliment. "I have spoken honestly, Mama." Bettina took a breath and turned to face her mother. "I am ready to face whatever consequences you deem appropriate for my behavior. Even if it is to wed someone of Father's choosing."

Jane licked her lips, wanting to say something in Bettina's defense, wanting to beg her mother not to marry Bettina off or arrange a situation for her simply because of her foolishness. Before she could do so, however, Lady Wilkinson pulled Bettina into a quick embrace.

"Rid yourself of such a foolish idea, my dear girl. If there had been any difficulty following your behavior, then there certainly would have been consequences. But since there are none, and since you have seen the foolishness of your ways, there is nothing we need to consider. Of course, I will be watching you a little more carefully now, but that is all I shall do."

Bettina immediately burst into sobs. Lady Wilkinson smiled at Jane, then at Lord Northwick, before turning her daughter and leading Bettina back along the hallway. Jane watched them for as long as she could before they turned a corner, still hearing her sister's sobs echoing back towards it.

They were alone again.

"It is over."

Lord Northwick slipped one hand around her waist as she spoke and, with great relief coursing through her, Jane turned herself into him so she might rest her head on his shoulder, feeling his chest rumble as he smiled down at her.

"At least I need have no concern that I am a particular favorite of your sister."

Her laughter bubbled out from the sheer happiness in knowing the matter was entirely brought to an end, joyous now she would have no further responsibility for Bettina, nor needed to fear that such a thing would happen again. There would be no requirement for her to watch Bettina closely on every occasion they went to, for the burden was now lifted from her shoulders – and how grateful Jane found herself. Now all she had to consider was her own heart.

"Miss Ainsley, we should continue walking."

Lord Northwick's voice held a warning and, with regret, Jane lifted her head and together, they began to meander along the hallway, giving the impression they were still hunting for this very important sprig of mistletoe they had been tasked to find - unless all of them had been fed.

"I can tell you are relieved."

A small sigh slipped from her. "I am. I confess I was

shocked to hear my sister had written such notes to other gentlemen also, but I am glad she chose to be honest. It was the right thing to do."

"An honesty we were sharing also, before we were interrupted." Lord Northwick's hand came to settle over hers, although he did not look in her direction. "There was something more to say, I think."

"Yes, I believe there was." Suddenly she could not seem to speak with any great strength, her stomach swirling madly as Lord Northwick finally looked towards her. Their steps slowed all the more until they were barely moving, with the air growing crisp and sharp around them as Jane waited for him to speak.

"I confess to you that I have found my own character altering significantly."

"Altering?" This was not the declaration she had expected, but Lord Northbrook nodded, his lips pulling into a light smile. "Yes. Altering. As I have said, I was a gentleman eager for nothing but delight. I had no plans to think of anything of my future, no intention of being honest with myself on what is required of me as a gentleman. I cared only about being entertained. My interests were brief and momentary, not realizing the significance and value of a deepening acquaintance." Taking a deep breath, he continued on, his words hurried. "When I say to you I have altered within myself, it is because my outlook on such things has changed so drastically that I do not think I am able to express the extent of it!"

Jane did not say a word, her mouth much too dry, her mind scrambling to make sense of what Lord Northwick expressed.

"It is because of you, Miss Ainsley." His voice was quieter now, his eyes finally searching for hers as he turned his head. "We have moved from those who wished to see nothing of each other to those who cannot seem to get enough of one another's company, have we not?" Coming to a complete stop, he turned all the more so he might look into her face. "At least I hope I do not speak for myself alone."

"No, indeed not, Lord Northwick." Despite her dry mouth, Jane responded quickly, her hand slipping from his arm so she might take both of his. "When I first arrived, I was determined to practically ignore you. And now, whenever I step into a room, I can do nothing but seek you out."

The truth did not seem hard to say. Rather, Jane recognized she *wanted* to tell him such things, wanted to be as honest as she could. "You say you are altered – do I not find myself altered also?"

Lord Northwick's tender smile seemed to light the hallway with bright sparks of joy as he lifted his hand from hers, only to run it along her cheek; his fingers brushing her neck, her shoulder, and then all the way down to catch her hand again. Jane shivered lightly at his touch, such heat burning through her as she had never before experienced. Everything in her desired to be closer to this gentleman, to share embraces and even kisses. She now understood what it was Bettina has been so desirous to experience for she felt the very same way – and it would only be satisfied if she might step into Lord Northwick's arms.

"You will not be angry with me then, if I tell you my feelings towards you have *also* altered significantly?"

"Angry?" Her exclamation echoed down the hallway and with embarrassment, she dropped her head only for Lord Northwick to move closer, his voice a soft murmur.

"It does me good to hear you speak so," he told her, his hands squeezing hers. "It brings my heart a great deal of joy."

"I could never be angry." Jane spoke carefully, but with great decisiveness. "I feel joy, happiness, gratitude, affection, but never anger. You are not the only one whose feelings have changed so drastically. I am *glad* they have. I am relieved, and I am filled with gratitude for all you have done."

Lord Northwick tilted his head to one side. "I fear my heart holds a little more for you than I have managed to express," he told her, his smile growing. "What would you say if I was to tell you I love you?"

Jane stared at him, her heart coming to a stop for just a moment. It was a more than astonishing to hear him speak so, more than she had ever thought would come from his lips. Struggling to find the right response and aware of the joyous roar in her heart, she struggled to find the right thing to say, only for her eyes to alight on something behind him.

With a lift of her finger to beg him to wait, she stepped away from him, going to the sideboard behind him and to the plant that sat on the top. Turning around to face him, she smiled brightly, holding the spring of mistletoe slightly above her head.

"I believe my answer would be *this*, Lord Northwick."

Lord Northwick's gaze went first to the mistletoe and then to her lips. With every fiber of her tingling with anticipation, she held it aloft until, after only two small steps, he was with her. His arms went around her, his head dropped to hers, and his kiss settled upon her lips, their hearts melding. Fire licked up from within her, sending swirls of smoke around her, confusing the rest of her senses. She felt herself melting, her arms around his neck, holding to him as though he was the only one who could support her. How long the kiss lasted she could not say, for it felt as though it were only a breath, and yet a whole hour gone at the same time. When

Lord Northwick lifted his head, Jane found she could not breathe for some moments thereafter.

"Your answer is very pleasing, my dear Jane." Lord Northwick's lips remained tantalizingly close to hers, and Jane could do nothing but think only of them. "It seems you have not only gained my heart, but you have also gained my lips as well."

"As you have also." She could only whisper, seeing the burning in his eyes and feeling the very same still smoldering within her. "I do love you also, Lord Northwick."

The mistletoe fell from her fingers as he wrapped his arms around her waist again, pulling her so tight against him that she did not think she would ever be able to separate from him. Nothing but joy and light filled her as she kissed the gentleman who possessed her heart and in whose heart she dwelled also.

I LOVE THE PARLOR GAMES, don't you? Bullet pudding! I am glad Lord Northwick and Jane found each other! Please check out another Christmas book A Family for Christmas while I am working on the next book in this series! Read ahead for a sneak peek!

The Returned Lords of Grosvenor Square
The Returned Lords of Grosvenor Square: A Regency
Romance Boxset
The Waiting Bride
The Long Return
The Duke's Saving Grace
A New Home for the Duke

The Spinsters Guild
The Spinsters Guild: A Sweet Regency Romance Boxset
A New Beginning
The Disgraced Bride
A Gentleman's Revenge
A Foolish Wager
A Lord Undone

Convenient Arrangements
Convenient Arrangements: A Regency Romance
Collection
A Broken Betrothal
In Search of Love
Wed in Disgrace
Betrayal and Lies
A Past to Forget
Engaged to a Friend

Landon House
Landon House: A Regency Romance Boxset
Mistaken for a Rake
A Selfish Heart
A Love Unbroken
A Christmas Match
A Most Suitable Bride

An Expectation of Love

Second Chance Regency Romance
Second Chance Regency Romance Boxset
Loving the Scarred Soldier
Second Chance for Love
A Family of her Own
A Spinster No More

Soldiers and Sweethearts
Soldiers and Sweethearts: A Sweet Regency Romance
Boxset
To Trust a Viscount
Whispers of the Heart
Dare to Love a Marquess
Healing the Earl
A Lady's Brave Heart

Ladies on their Own: Governesses and Companions
More Than a Companion
The Hidden Governess
The Companion and the Earl
More than a Governess
Protected by the Companion
A Wager with a Viscount

Lost Fortunes, Found Love
A Viscount's Stolen Fortune
For Richer, For Poorer

Christmas Stories

Christmas Kisses (Series)

The Lady's Christmas Kiss
A Viscount's Christmas Queen

Love and Christmas Wishes: Three Regency Romance
Novellas
A Family for Christmas
Mistletoe Magic: A Regency Romance
Heart, Homes & Holidays: A Sweet Romance Anthology

Happy Reading!

All my love,

Rose

A SNEAK PEEK OF A FAMILY
FOR CHRISTMAS

It seemed strange, on such a somber occasion as a funeral, that there were boughs of holly, hundreds of candles and garlands of evergreens decorating the church ready for the service to commemorate the beginning of Advent that was due to take place the next day. Anna Campbell looked at the coffin set upon trestles at the altar. It contained the mortal remains of her father, Colin Campbell. The casket was the best she could afford—and had been the cheapest the carpenter could offer. Anna ran a hand over the rough, unvarnished wood and wondered if she would miss him at all.

The vicar's words echoed around the empty church as he performed the final blessing and said a solemn prayer commending Pa to God's mercy. He gave Anna a rueful smile, then nodded to the men hovering at the very back of the church to come and fetch the coffin to take it to the gravesite. They were clad in dark clothes, their boots and breeches covered with mud. They had swarthy complexions from working outside in all weathers. Their expressions were solemn and inscrutable. She could only assume that they were the gravediggers and that the vicar had paid them a few coppers more to come and carry Pa to the gravesite as she had nobody who might do it for her. She nodded to them politely, and they gave her a respectful half-bow, then another to the casket, before they picked it up and began to walk steadily down the aisle.

Anna followed them, the vicar walking just ahead of them all as they carried her father's body towards the doors of the church. The pews were all empty. There was not a soul present to witness Pa's passing or to offer Anna their love and support. It did not surprise Anna that not even one of the more dedicated members of the congregation had come, as they often would for even a stranger that was to be buried. Pa had made too many enemies in his life for anyone to mourn him, much less offer him respect, and she hadn't known if there was anyone she should have told that he had finally succumbed to the evils his whoring, drinking, and gambling had put upon his body. She doubted that even she would miss him.

There was an aunt somewhere. Anna's mother's sister. There had been no contact between them since long before Anna had been born, so she doubted that even they, her only family now, would have wanted to come and pay their respects. Pa had always grumbled that Mama's high-and-mighty sister had never thought Pa good enough—it had always been clear that there was little love lost between them. All Anna knew of Aunt Hannah was her mother's stories of their childhood and the moments when it was clear just how much she missed her sister after Hannah had upped and left home to marry a man who lived in some grand city somewhere. It might have been London, or Liverpool, York, or even Edinburgh. It had never been spoken of, and Anna had been too young to remember the details—Ma had died when Anna was barely five years old, and all she had been left with was an idea that someday she might seek out her aunt so that she could get away from her miserable life with Pa.

The silent quartet made their way out of the church. The weather was mild but damp, making everything smell just a little earthy. The churchyard was sheltered by trees and filled with extravagant monuments to the much-beloved dead. Anna admired the beauty of some of the carvings and sculptures that adorned the graves of the wealthy, buried as close to the church as they could be. She noted the way the extravagance of the closest graves gave way to simple headstones and unadorned crosses as they moved further away from the hallowed vaults of the imposing village church. But they kept on walking. Anna could not afford even as much as had been provided by these families of more modest means. Pa would be buried in a quiet corner, along with many other men who died penniless in recent weeks, with no grave marker of any kind. He would be forgotten by the world.

With a grimace, she thought about the debts her father had left behind. Some she would be able to forget, as they were many years old and it would be unlikely that she would ever see those of her father's creditors again. Many would simply acknowledge that her father could no longer pay and so would consider the debts null and void. But there were too many that would expect her to make good on them, despite knowing she hadn't a sous to her name. Anna had no idea how she would ever make payment of such vast sums, and she feared that she would be followed wherever she might go by some very unsavory characters.

The gravediggers made their way through the churchyard to a boggy corner that was the furthest from the church that was possible and lowered the coffin into the gaping hole in the ground. Inside the hole, Anna could see a number of other rough coffins and even a couple of bodies wrapped in nothing more than a sheet of rough cloth. It made her sad to think that so many men and women ended their days in such a manner, cheek by jowl with people they had not even known. She wondered briefly if like Pa, they deserved such an ignominious end, or if they had been the unfortunate victims of poverty and sickness. She could only hope that what the bible taught was true, that man's earthly remains mattered little—that it was the soul that God cared about. Even for Pa, she prayed that he had done enough good in his life, somewhere, and had repented of his many sins so he might be permitted to enter heaven's gates.

The vicar sprinkled holy water over the grave, said a brief prayer of committal, and it was over. The gravediggers began to shovel the earth piled up beside the grave back into the hole, and the vicar made his way back inside the church —once Anna had handed him a small purse with all the coin she had left in the world. She'd had to sell Pa's wagon and everything in it just to give him this meager funeral. Even men of God needed to be paid their share.

Anna stood at the graveside and watched until the last shovelful of earth was back where it had come from and the gravediggers had moved away. "You got what you deserved," she said bitterly, remembering the beatings she'd gotten over the years. Pa had always been handy with his fists when in his cups, and he had been a sore loser. Anna had always been to blame for everything that had gone wrong in Pa's life, from saddling him with her very presence, to the times when a horse trade fell through because she'd fallen off the half-wild mounts he insisted on selling before they were ready. "But you were all I had, and so I am glad I have done right by you. Rest easy in your grave, Pa."

She walked away, her head held high. Anna had learned early that she needed to hide her feelings and to pretend to be that which she was not. Pa made her play so many roles as part of his many schemes and she'd learned young how to mimic those around her. Now, perhaps those skills would help her to move on and to find a better life. Anna knew that she could speak more eloquently than most of her kind, and she moved with grace. She was sure that she would be able to find a position in a fine house some-where – even if she had to start at the bottom as a scullery maid or kitchen hand. Anna knew how to work hard – even if Pa never had.

She made her way back to the grand porch of the church and picked up the old carpetbag she had left there. Inside its battered, capacious exterior was everything Anna possessed. A tattered gown and clean undergarments, an old necklace Pa swore had belonged to her mother and a book of poetry she'd found in amongst her mother's old things some years earlier. Anna could barely read them, though she tried hard to do so. She could vaguely remember her mother reading them to her, but the recollection was so hazy and vague Anna often wondered if she'd simply imag-ined it.

Anna felt that she had known no other life than the one she had shared with Pa, though she knew that things had been very different whilst her mother had been alive. In her memories, Ma was always so much more refined than Pa, she had interests and skills that he had grown to be envious of, sparking his temper and spite. Anna often wondered how differently her life might have been had Ma lived longer. Perhaps she'd be able to read and write, have taken up a place in service and be respectable.

Instead, a life of trading in half-wild horses, card-sharping, and moving from town to town before anyone could catch Pa and demand he repay them had not given Anna many usable skills, other than the ability to act to deceive. She did not wish to continue in the vein that he had followed. His passing was her chance to make a new life, one where she could do good rather than harm. Yet there were few employers that would take on an unskilled, uneducated, and penniless woman such as herself. She'd probably end up having to throw herself on the mercy of the parish, though she vowed to do all she could to avoid such an outcome.

With a last glance at the church, bedecked with greenery for the Christmas celebrations, Anna turned and made her way out onto the street. As she passed through the lychgate, she vowed never to look back. There must be a way that she could turn her life around. There had to be someone or somewhere that she could go where she would not only be welcomed, but she would be useful and could make enough money to support herself. But it would not be here, not in this miserable little village where the chain that bound her had finally been buried.

Feeling more than a little trepidatious, Anna turned left out of the gate, putting Sparsholt behind her, and began to walk along the rutted road that would lead her first to Winchester and then onwards towards Farnham and Guildford. She prayed that there would be some work for her in one of these places, but if there were not, then she would continue onwards towards London. It was the wrong time of year to be searching for work; employers were often too caught up with arranging their Christmas celebrations for family and friends to be doing much business, but she had no choice.

A glimmer of blue began to appear between the clouds in the sky above as she walked briskly along the road to Winchester. Anna couldn't help but feel optimistic as the day progressed and the sun finally appeared, bathing her face in its light and gentle winter warmth. The death of her father would have made her sad, had he been the kind of father one actually mourned. With him gone, Anna now had the opportunity to create her own life in the way she wished. It would be hard work, and she knew that she would need a lot of luck, too—yet she knew, deep within, that life would get better for her.

As the miles passed, and the sun disappeared behind ominous gray clouds once more, Anna's pace slowed, and her optimism faded. Her feet were riddled with blisters, her shoulders and arms ached from carrying her bag—even though she had shifted it from one hand to the other every half a mile or so—and she was bone-tired. She couldn't see so much as a shack anywhere along the road, and it was nearing nightfall. Anna began to fear that she might not find a safe place to stay for the night, so she tried unsuccessfully to pick up her pace once more. The pain in her sore feet was excruciating. "Ow," she moaned aloud. "What possessed me to think this was ever a good idea?"

Turning to look behind her, hopeful that she might see a carriage, or even a cart heading her way, Anna sighed heavily. There had been no passing traffic on the road all day, in either direction, and she could see no movement on the horizon now. She trudged on as the light grew dimmer, her pride and will sapped from the long day's walk and the prospect of a night alone by the roadside with nothing to keep her warm or fill her belly. She stopped by the side of the road and perched on a milestone that told her she only had another three miles until she reached Winchester. She could be there in two hours, maybe even less than that if she could forget how much her feet hurt and walk faster. It would be after dark, but at least she would be surrounded by houses and inns. Someone would surely be kind enough to take her in if she offered her services, cooking and cleaning, in return for a bed?

Wearily, she stood up, stretched, fidgeted her feet a little in her boots, grimacing at the discomfort, and then set off once more. Her progress was slow, and she winced with every step, but she kept pushing on. "I'll be there in no time," she repeated to herself over and over again—wishing with her every breath that it were true. She couldn't have traveled more than another half a mile when there was, finally, the sound of hooves and wheels coming along the road behind her.

Anna stopped and turned around. A large black shape was hurtling along the road, rocking and swaying as it fairly flew over the potholes and ruts in the road. The driver on the box was clad all in black, and he was whipping up his team of two with loud cries and rapid cracks of his whip. He didn't look to have seen her, so Anna stepped into the road a little and waved her hands wildly, praying he would stop and take her into Winchester. But as the carriage approached, Anna could see that he had no intention of stopping. The driver did not quit urging his horses onwards, and the phaeton approached her at a reckless speed.

Anna tried to step back out of the way, but her left heel caught in her skirts. Normally, she would have been more than capable of coping with such a mishap, but she was so weary that her balance seemed to have deserted her and she fell, tumbling into a ditch by the side of the road. She fell heavily onto the knee of the leg that was caught up in her skirt, and she heard a sickening crack as her body finally came to rest. She clutched at her leg and moaned. The pain was excruciating, and she tried to get up. She sobbed, though no tears fell onto her cheeks. It was as if her body was too tired even to do that.

Nobody would ever find her here; she hadn't seen the ditch from the road herself, so she couldn't expect anyone else passing to see it—to see her. If she could at least get back onto the road, somebody might pass by. All she had left was hope, and there was precious little of that available to her—but she must do all she could to at least try to be seen, to be rescued. She pushed herself up on her weary arms and tried to grab hold of some of the wet grass on the bank to pull herself to her feet, but before she'd even tried to put weight on her bad leg, she collapsed back to the ground with a piercing scream.

"How am I ever to get out of here?" she moaned as she cradled her leg once again, and the tears finally began to fall. "I could die here. I must not be so weak. If I have to drag myself out of this dratted ditch, then that is what I must do." Taking a deep breath, she began to claw her way up the bank. The aches in her arms, her shoulders, and her back had been bothering her all day, but they had been nothing to the ferocious burning in her muscles now. Anna gritted her teeth, growling and screaming as she needed to, in order to get herself back onto the road. She was breathless and spent when she finally made it. Her head dropped to the floor, her chest heaving with the exertion, her body paralyzed by the pain that seemed to have taken over every part of her. She had done what she could. It would be up to God and the Fates to decide if it were enough.

CHAPTER TWO

"She threw a glass of wine in my face and told me, quite rightly, that she never wished to see me again," Edward, Lord Westerham said with a grin, leaning back against the plushly upholstered seats in his godmother's luxurious landau as they made their way to Winchester for Sunday Mass. His audience reacted as they so often did when he recanted the tales of his misdeeds. His father, opposite, smirked with suppressed amusement; his mother, sat beside her husband, gave him a look of exasperation; and his godmother, sat beside him, gave a resoundingly contagious belly laugh. He laughed with her as she patted his hand fondly. She always loved his stories of his exploits in London.

"Dear Edward, I sometimes wonder if we shall ever see you happily wed," Lady Frances, Countess Tremaine said, tucking an arm through his and winking at him. He knew she did not mind if he ever settled down, as long as he was happy.

Lady Tremaine was what most people would call a character, Edward supposed. Eccentric, clever as anyone he'd ever met, and always quick to think and act, she did not care much for convention and certainly didn't seem to mind that he showed little evidence of settling down—unlike his mother, Lady Frances' oldest and dearest friend.

The two women had grown up together and had been firm friends for as long as they could remember. They had learned to ride together, to embroider and all of the other ladylike arts—though to hear them tell it, Mama had often undertaken such tasks for Lady Tremaine so that she might bury her head in the books from her father's library. Edward had never met two people so very different, from their habits and interests to their physical appearance. It often made him wonder how their friendship had lasted so long.

Mama was tall and thin with a very patrician manner. Societal mores were important to her, and Edward doubted if she had ever set a foot out of line in her forty-nine years. She was a perfect lady, from her elegant posture to her dainty manners. She drew and painted beautiful watercolors, played the pianoforte with adequate skill and feeling, and sang like a lark. She never argued with Edward's father, or anyone else for that matter. She was docile and did as she was expected, was the perfect hostess, and was never late to anything.

In stark contrast, Lady Frances was short and plump. She lived life on her terms. She drank port and smoked cigars—often refusing to leave the dinner table after supper in order to remain with the men and discuss politics and economics rather than retire to the drawing-room along with the other women. She talked knowledgeably about running her estates, the country's affairs, and could drink as heartily as any man. She was argumentative and stubborn— usually because she was so often right. She eschewed the ladylike arts, preferring to focus on what was going on in the world around her. She ran her home the way she pleased, and heaven help any man who tried to tell her otherwise. And, to her mind, punctuality was something that only ever applied to other people. Edward adored her.

Mama pursed her lips. "I do wish you would learn to be a little more circumspect, Edward," she said. "You are getting quite the reputation for being a flirt."

"Oh, Mama, do speak plainly," Edward said with a grin, knowing that she would never say what she truly thought of his behavior. "I am rapidly heading towards being known as a bounder and a cad."

"I did not say that, Edward," Mama said with a frown. "Nor would I ever say such a thing. I hope that no child of mine would ever be even considered to be such a thing. Why can you not see that people even implying them is most detrimental to your good character?"

"Simply because it is not true," Edward assured her. "I cannot be responsible for the ways other people might think of me, nor do I wish to be, Mama. I may possibly have let Lady Allingham think I cared more for her than I did, but I did not entirely deserve to have wine thrown in my face. I was a gentleman at all times. I cannot be held responsible for that silly ninny's thinking I was about to propose marriage simply because I was kind enough to dance with her once and take her to supper at Almack's."

"He's quite right, Harriet," Papa said, looking up briefly from his newspaper. "The boy cannot be expected to know the intentions of every filly that he dances with, nor should he try. Young girls these days, they all seem to think that every man must be after them just because they have a pretty face and a dowry. In my day, well, things were different."

"Of course they were, Harold," Lady Tremaine said,

rolling her eyes. "Matches were made by our parents, as they should be. And nobody ever married for love, or attraction, or tried to wheedle their way out of a match made for them by their father. We accepted our fate and married whether we liked the person or not—and we made the very best of it we could." Her words were dripping with sarcasm. Edward had to try very hard to maintain a straight face. Papa hated to be wrong and hated it even more when it was Lady Tremaine making him feel small, though he often gave her such easy opportunities to do so.

"Now you are just being argumentative, Frances," Papa said. "You know full well what I meant. Decisions just weren't made on such silly nonsense as how a girl felt when she danced with a chap."

"And it led to so many happy marriages," Lady Tremaine said with a dramatic swoon and a heavy sigh. She giggled, unable to maintain her composure. "Too many women, like myself, Harold, ended up wed to idiots because of the old ways. I'm not saying that things have improved any—but I do think that getting to know the man you are to wed and being sure you like him first isn't such a silly idea as you think."

"But things haven't really changed," Edward said thoughtfully. "Even though it appears that there is a choice, there really isn't for many young people today. They are pushed towards matches with people that are deemed suitable. They must have a title and wealth. They must dance well and look pretty. One's parents still have to approve a match or both men and women face being disinherited. It may appear that there is more choice, but I don't think there is."

Papa nodded his agreement. "And that is why every young girl is simply falling at Edward's feet, because he is

Lord Westerham, will one day become Earl of Winterton. He has a fine estate, will inherit an even better one, and has good standing in Society. He dresses well and is handsome —and has a fortune many would be envious of. He will inherit my seat in Parliament and is friends with Prinny. Any young woman in Society is going to be pushed—by her mother and father, no less—to ensnare him."

"I don't disagree," Mama said, now frowning at them all. "But I do think that because of that, Edward needs to be more circumspect in the manner in which he behaves. It does our family name no good to have him labeled as some bounder."

"Mama, I truly do not think that I will be," Edward assured her, reaching across the carriage to take her hand. "I am respectful, and I am polite. I flirt a little, but no more than any man should. I do not ever promise a girl anything I cannot or will not deliver. I cannot be held responsible for the silliness that they attach to those things in the privacy of their bedchambers. I can assure you that I have no intention of bringing the family name into disrepute." He lifted her hand to his lips and kissed her hand tenderly.

She sighed and reached out with her free hand to caress his cheek. "I do wish, sometimes, that you weren't so handsome or charming. It will be your undoing, my darling boy."

"I shall do my best to be sure it will not," Edward said solemnly, then leaned back in his seat once more.

Edward glanced out of the carriage as the conversation lulled. The carriage wasn't going very fast, as the driver was having to be extremely careful where he let the horses go. The weather in recent days had been wet and miserable. The roads were rutted, and the ditches and some of the fields on either side of the road were filled with water from the heavy rainfall overnight. It always surprised him to see what had once been green and verdant become a lake so swiftly. The flooding made the land exceptionally fertile, but it made choosing the right crops for such land more challenging for the men who made their living from it.

They passed a couple of men trudging by the side of the road, pickaxes and shovels in hand. They were clearly trying to unblock the channels that allowed the water to drain from the road into the ditches and then onwards into the streams and rivers. Their faces were streaked with mud, their clothes sodden. Edward couldn't help feeling grateful that he was warm and dry inside the coach rather than out there in the inclement weather having to work so hard.

As they neared Winchester, there were more people on the roads, some clad in their Sunday best, others dressed for work as if it were any other day. All of them seemed to be ignoring what seemed to be a large pile of old clothes that had been left by the wayside. Edward stared at them wondering why anyone would have done such a thing. Something twitched, making the bundle move ever so slightly. Edward blinked and rubbed at his eyes, sure he must have been imagining it. The rain was coming down quite heavily again, the sound of the raindrops a cascade on the roof of the coach. The view through the carriage window was a little blurred. But when he looked back, Edward was certain that the bundle had moved again.

Perhaps it was just a rat, or something of that ilk, rummaging around to see if there was anything it might eat or that it might make use of for its nest, but Edward wasn't so sure. He banged his silver-topped cane on the roof of the carriage to tell the driver to stop. "Edward?" his mother asked, clearly surprised that he should do such a thing when they hadn't yet reached the church.

"I think there might be someone out there, by the side of

the road," Edward said as the carriage came to a halt and he jumped out of the door.

He hurried to where the bundle lay. As he drew closer, it was quite clear that it was a person, though their leg was poking out at a most peculiar angle. He wondered why nobody else had seemed even to see it. Those on foot were just walking by, shielding their faces from the rain. He supposed they were only in a hurry to get out of the cold and wet weather, so had little time to look around them, but it seemed strange to him that they could walk by someone in need.

Kneeling beside the body, the mud soaked through Edward's breeches. It was cold as ice and chilled him to the bone. Edward shuddered. To have met your end in such a way, in the mud, alone, was simply horrific to his mind. Edward rolled the body over and gasped.

The face that looked up at him was that of a young woman, her hair and clothes utterly caked in mud. Her skin, between the brown streaks, was as pale as milk. She was cold as ice, and her body was stiff and unyielding, as though she were dead, but Edward could see a tiny rise and fall in her chest. "It's a young woman. She's badly hurt—but she's alive," he cried out as his father clambered out of the carriage and made his way towards him.

Yes, it is Anna! What will happen to her? Check out the rest of the story in the Kindle Store! A Family for Christmas

www.ingramcontent.com/pod-product-compliance
Lightning Source LLC
Chambersburg PA
CBHW071320140726
47996CB00005B/1746